VICE SQUAD COP

VICE SQUAD COP

MICHAEL CAREY

CUTTING EDGE

ISBN-13: 978-1-962896-65-8

Published by
Cutting Edge Books
PO Box 8212
Calabasas, CA 91372
www.cuttingedgebooks.com

FOR:

Elizabeth and Jeffrey

CHAPTER ONE

ASSISTANT CHIEF Inspector Mike Rossetti's office smelled rancidly of stale cigar smoke and rotted wood. The one tiny, moisture-streaked window was closed tight and the pale yellow overhead light was on.

Steve Hochuli sat uncomfortably on a small wooden chair, feeling big and buffalo-like in his stiff blue uniform with its clean wooden smell, its shiny brass buttons and silver shield. He shifted uncomfortably in the chair and the steel-linked nippers pinged against the brass whistle attached to his gun-belt.

Chief Rossetti was talking into the telephone in a deep, confident voice. He was a stubby, thick-necked man with heavy shoulders and an open, ruddy face. He was completely bald except for two locks of hair, dyed black, which were plastered carefully across the top of his scalp. His eyes were distortedly large and brown under glass.

The Chief hung up the phone abruptly and addressed himself to Steve with deceptive frankness.

"Know what they call me around here, Hochuli?"

"No, sir."

The open, ruddy face broke into a good-natured grin.

"The whip. I'm the big whip."

The Chief was short and burly and no longer young. It was as though an awareness of age had not yet come to him. He was too alert, over stimulated, unable to relax.

Steve stirred uneasily. The office was close and airless. The Chief's face loomed in front of him.

"Too hot in here for you?"

"A little."

"For Christ's sake," the Chief exploded. "Take that damned overcoat off and relax. You're no prisoner."

Steve removed the coat and hung it where the Chief indicated.

"Here," the Chief tossed him a package of cigarettes. "Smoke. Relax. What the hell's wrong with you?"

"Tensed up, I guess, Chief."

"Untense then."

Steve lit a cigarette and leaned back on his chair.

"That's better," the Chief said, nodding and studying Steve.

The Chief's manner changed abruptly. He scowled and placed a yellow pad and pencil on his desk.

"All right," he said, "let's get down to business."

The freshly sharpened pencil was poised in the stubby fingers.

"Rank, name, shield number and command?"

"Patrolman Steve Hochuli, Shield 84, 145 Precinct."

The Chief scribbled diligently on the pad.

"Age?"

"Twenty-seven."

"How long on the force?"

"Three years."

"Interested in plain-clothes work?"

"Yes, sir."

"Know what that means?"

"Yes, sir. The Vice Squad."

The Vice Squad, Steve thought, the most interesting assignment in the Police Department and also the most dangerous. Men didn't simply get dropped from a detail like this. Very often they went to jail. He was crazy to want it.

The Chief's deep voice droned on.

"Get any departmental complaints in the past?"

"None."

"Any complaints pending right now?"

"None."

"Married?"

"No, sir."

"Go to church regularly?"

"As often as I can, Chief."

The Chief grinned his flat grin and nodded understandingly. A cop's hours weren't always conducive to church going.

"Any objections to making prostitution arrests?"

The idea was distasteful to him. Yet he wanted the detail and if arresting prostitutes was part of it he would have to go along.

"No objections, sir."

The overhead light reflected in the Chief's glasses as he lit a cigar and puffed clouds of blue smoke across the desk.

"Drink much, Hochuli?"

"No, sir."

"Own your own home?"

"No, sir. I rent a four room apartment in the Bronx."

"How much rent you pay?"

"Forty a month."

"Got a car?"

"Yes, sir."

"Paid for?"

"Yes, sir."

"Any outstanding debts?"

"None."

"How much money you got in the bank?"

"Seven hundred dollars."

"What schooling you got?"

"Two years of college."

"Where?"

"Columbia."

"Any other source of income?"

"No, sir. Just my salary."

The Chief leaned back in his swivel chair.

"Suppose you're wondering why I'm asking all these questions?" he said, staring at the ceiling.

"It's a kind of screening, isn't it?" Steve volunteered.

"Right," the Chief agreed, nodding his big head. "But it's more than that."

He held up a sheet of paper in his heavy, spatulated fingers.

"Know what this is?" he said, dramatically.

"No, sir."

"Your pedigree sheet. You filled it out more than three years ago at the Police Academy."

Steve felt secure. Go ahead and check, Chief, he thought. I've given you straight answers all the way.

"We don't take just any cop for the Headquarters Vice Squad. You got to be sharp and you got to be honest. Got to have a head on your shoulders for this work. Not every man is suited to it."

Forget the speeches, Steve thought, let's get this over with.

"My second reason," the Chief was saying, checking off two fingers methodically, "is that we have a permanent record on file here in this office in case you get called up by the District Attorney. Then you can refer to it and refresh your memory."

The Chief's voice went suddenly hoarse and angry. "Don't look so God-damned dumb," he shouted. "You know as well as I do any time the D.A. wants to make Judge he picks on the Vice Squad. He lops off the heads of a couple of cops; the newspapers scream headlines; the good citizens treat him to testimonial dinners and pretty soon he's got his appointment to the bench. Understand?"

"I think so, Chief," Steve said, hesitantly. He wished Rossetti would stop lecturing.

"You will, Hochuli. *You will*."

Steve made a move to rise. He felt the interview was over.

"Sit down!" the Chief rasped. "I'll let you know when I want to get rid of you. Know anything about gambling?"

"Yes, sir."

"Ever do any investigating work?"

"Yes, sir, during the war."

"What kind of investigating was it?"

Steve took a deep breath and launched into it. "Well," he said, quietly, "sometimes the men on the merchant vessels would sell cigarettes or clothing or exchange money in the black markets of Europe and Africa. It was our job to apprehend them and take their papers away so they couldn't sail any more."

"Get many convictions?"

"Yes, sir, about ninety per cent."

"You have a rank in the service?"

"Lieutenant j.g. in the Coast Guard."

The Chief seemed impressed for the first time.

"You studying for the Sergeant's Test coming up?"

"Yes, I am."

He had in fact been studying for the test for the past six months, attending lectures at the Police Academy and a private school twice a week.

"If you're going to be a boss in this department you need the Vice Squad background," the Chief said, soberly. "Teach you how to gather evidence and make arrests. Teach you how to testify in court too so that you don't make an ass of yourself."

The Chief nodded his big head portentously.

"Ever go into the black market yourself while you were overseas?" the Chief snapped suddenly.

"My job was to apprehend the merchant sailors who went into the black market," he said, slowly and quietly. "I never went into it myself. The salary I made was adequate for my needs."

The Chief grinned and bit off the end of a large cigar, spitting the wad of tobacco to the floor. He looked as pleased with himself as the proverbial Cheshire cat. He lit the cigar and stared gravely at Steve. Suddenly he grunted and picked up the new yellow pencil on his desk. He turned it end over end several times deep in thought. The distorted eyes behind the glasses suddenly twinkled.

"Give you a rough time, Hochuli?"

"You did, Chief."

"Don't let it get you down."

Steve grinned.

The Chief studied the calendar on his desk.

"Tomorrow's Tuesday. You report up here Wednesday morning at ten to Lt. Quinlan. He's my Supervisor of Plain-clothes."

"Right, Chief," Steve said, rising and shrugging into the heavy uniform overcoat.

"I think you'll turn out all right," The Chief said, offering his hand.

"Thank you, Chief."

They shook hands briefly and Steve headed for the door.

"Hey, Hochuli," the Chief called. "Remember—report up here in plain-clothes."

"Yes, sir."

Steve closed the door quietly behind him.

CHAPTER TWO

THE PLACE was the cocktail lounge of a minor hotel complete with dim lights, bad food and a piano player who kept banging out popular tunes with the desperation of a wornout automaton. The dim lights hid the worn spots in the frowzy purple velvet hangings and black cigarette burns in the blue carpeting. The blue paint on the walls was blistered and peeling. There was the smell of stale tobacco, liquor, and cheap, perfumed deodorant.

Steve sat with his partner, Jerry Brickley, in one of the booths that ran in a narrow line from the bar to the grease-smelling kitchen. Both men were dressed in navy uniforms.

Jerry was a tall, loose limbed man with a small handsome face and a lean head, set closely with curly black hair. He was twenty-five. He spoke in a nervous voice that now and again was blurred with an airy lisp. He was full of the most unhesitating and annoying self-confidence.

He and Steve were working on a prostitute referred to in the police complaint simply as "Rusty" who frequented this dive. Navy men were her pet prey.

After a week of waiting they had spotted her. For three nights running they had watched her. She always entered alone around eleven o'clock and invariably left with her navy man by one. If there were no men in uniform in the lounge she left alone without trying to pick up anyone. She never sat at the tables. Evidently she didn't believe in spending her money on tips for the waiters but only on drinks. She went from cheap straight drinks to mixed, expensive ones when she picked up a customer.

"It's ten-thirty now," Steve said, glancing at his wristwatch. "Hope she shows tonight."

"She'll show," Jerry said, grinning his tight, sly grin.

Steve gulped down his rye and soda. He had read the police books and the social studies books pointing out the great need for taking prostitutes off the streets but, somehow, he couldn't bring himself to believe that prostitution, as such, was morally wrong. If a girl wanted voluntarily to follow that way of life and she was clean and cautious he could think of no reason why she shouldn't be allowed to live as she pleased. He wished he could have Jerry's self-righteous approach to the case.

Steve blurted out suddenly. "You make the arrest, Jerry."

Two bright, angry spots appeared in Jerry's pale face. He shook his head slowly. "Not me, Stevie boy," he said, slowly, controlling his anger. "She's all yours." He began enumerating his reasons. "First, it's your complaint. Second, you're a bachelor, and third, I don't know a thing about the navy, in case she starts asking questions about ships and sealing wax."

"All right," Steve said, nodding ruefully. "I'd better get over to the bar before she comes. You wait outside in the car. If I make contact I'll take her wherever she wants to go in a cab." He placed his hand on Jerry's shoulder. "And you stay close to us," he said. "And don't get lost."

"You sound frightened, Steve," Jerry laughed.

"I am. My first prostitution pinch and I'm not happy about it."

"I'll be right on your tail all the way," Jerry reassured him.

Steve moved to the bar, ordered another drink and waited. As he waited he continued to drink. His face began to stiffen and he grinned at himself in the bar mirror. He looked waxen in the dull light of the bar. He would have to pretend he liked this girl well enough to go to bed with her. He tried to smile at his reflection in the mirror but without success.

The large clock over the cash register with its circling fluid light indicated eleven-ten. Perhaps she wouldn't show tonight after all. He wished the whole thing were over and done with and envied Jerry sitting out there in the car out of the whole messy business. He ordered another drink and stared dumbly at the shiny, colored bottles of liquor lined up behind the bar.

And then she was in the bar, coming toward him. Slender, oddly elfin with piquant blue eyes, very white skin and elegantly made; a very pretty girl with a tiny nose, red hair and a strangely twisted white smile. There was no professional hardness about her. Perhaps he was mistaken about her after all. If he weren't mistaken unpleasant things were going to happen to her.

If only she weren't so damnably pretty and girlish looking.

"Hello," she said, smiling up at him and sitting down on the next stool.

"Hello," he replied, twirling his glass between his thumb and index finger. "Time for a refill. Want a drink?"

She hadn't recognized him. For three nights he had watched her and she hadn't noticed him at all. The navy uniform was magic.

"Sure," she murmured. "Scotch and soda, please."

The bartender poured two.

"Been in port long?" she said, touching glasses with him.

"Not long."

"My name's Rusty."

"Steve," he said, quietly.

Her voice was soft and light. "You look tired," she said.

"Long trip. Big ocean out there."

"Not much fun out at sea all the time," she said, smiling at him.

"No fun at all," he agreed.

She must be twenty-one or two, he thought.

"It's awfully unfair," she was saying.

She was mannered, affected, and full of curiosity. Perhaps that was the trademark of her profession. That and loads of sympathetic understanding. The books all said girls who went in for prostitution were a dull, lazy lot. This girl didn't fit into that category at all.

"Awfully unfair to you men," she repeated, smiling at him again.

"What?" he said. "What's awfully unfair?"

"You men out on those ships all the time without any women."

"Very unnatural life," he agreed, smiling back at her. She had him believing his story and feeling sorry for himself.

Her broad white forehead wrinkled and she stared into the bubbling glass in front of her.

"Don't you miss us women when you're out at sea?"

"Sure," he said, lighting a cigarette. "Very much."

She helped herself to a cigarette from the pack he left on the bar. He lit it for her. She inhaled deeply and wafted the smoke lazily through her nostrils. She had a beautiful, white, slender throat.

"You don't like to talk, do you?" she said.

"To a pretty girl any time," he countered, with a dismal attempt at gallantry.

"You frighten me a little."

"Why?" he said, smiling disarmingly.

"I don't know," she said. Her piquant blue eyes were out of focus now. "I think you could be real tough if you wanted to."

"Not me," he said, laughing.

Suddenly she reached out and touched him. It was a strange gesture. She was feeling for his gun. The place where it would be hanging in a shoulder holster. Only he was left-handed and the gun was on the other side. Real professional gesture that. She was suspicious all right. Not nearly as naïve or innocent as she looked.

"What was that for?" he said, forcing a laugh.

"I'm impulsive," she said, frowning and puffing on her cigarette. "You sure you're not a cop?"

"Sure," he said, flatly. "Don't even like cops."

"Oh," she said thoughtfully. "They're not bad guys."

He ordered another round of drinks and ignored her, staring at a pretty brunette sitting alone at the other end of the bar.

"Pretty, isn't she," Rusty said, moving closer and smiling up at him demandingly.

"No comparison," he said, quickly. "Not in your league at all."

"You're nice," she said.

"We're both nice," he said, lifting his glass. "Let's drink to it."

She drank and laughed, with her funny, crooked mouth, neatly made up with bright orange-red lipstick. What in hell was a kid like this doing kicking around the bars of the city taking men on?

"I'm a model," she volunteered.

"You are? What do you model?"

"Brassieres," she confided, giggling.

"I believe you," he said, staring at the full breasts under the pale green dress.

"Stop staring at me like that."

And then she threw back her head and laughed recklessly, invitingly—a white-toothed, open-city kind of a laugh. She made him think of wartime Paris, or Rome on a sunny spring day. In a way she was like an open city in the midst of some complex war. But he must tread softly in this open city. One false move and the city would be closed tight.

"I like sailors," she said, softly, brushing her knee against him.

"I'm glad," he said, staring at his drink.

This was it. Soon she would make her play.

"Why?"

"Because I'm a sailor and you must like me."

"I do," she said, leaning over and brushing her lips against his cheek.

He was surprised that he considered this prostitute so exciting, but under any other conditions she would be very easy to like.

He wondered why that was. Perhaps the movies and the newspapers—or was it the war? War made prostitution legal and necessary and acceptable. You don't think about it, but then, suddenly you're a cop and have to arrest prostitutes and you realize that unconsciously you have been accepting the idea of prostitution as an almost normal accompaniment of everyday city life.

He almost had a compulsion to tell her he was a cop and that she had better take off. That he would be compelled to arrest her if she made one wrong move began to overwhelm him.

In wartime Paris or Rome or Marseilles such a relationship was commonplace, but here in the States it was wrong—legally and morally wrong. He was going to hurt this girl, deprive her of her liberty, her freedom, and he didn't even know her. Had not even seen her harm a single soul.

"You look very handsome," she was saying, smiling up at him.

Her eyes were very blue and soft.

"I like men," she said, leaning against him. "I really like men."

He threw back his head and laughed. One or two of the curious people draped over the bar stared bleakly at them for a moment and then returned to their drinks.

He ordered another round. She teasingly ran long, pale fingers through the short, dark hairs that covered the back of his hand.

"My, but you have strong hands," she said, wrinkling her nose at him.

"My, but you have a tiny nose," he mimicked reaching toward her as though to steal it away—the way you might do with a very small child.

Her eyes went bright and she clasped both his hands in hers. She glanced quickly at her wristwatch. It was almost one o'clock.

"Let's leave here," she whispered.

"Why?" he said.

"You look like you could use some fun."

"What do you mean?"

The police manual stated you had to get them to explain themselves in more definite language so you could use the statement against them in court.

"You know what fun is?"

"No. Tell me."

"Well," she said, childishly. "If you pay me enough I'll go to bed with you."

There it was. Blunt and simple. The statement was there but alone it wasn't enough to make a pinch.

"Just like that?" he said, trying to grin naturally.

"Yes," she said, lowering her eyes. Her hand pressed against him hungrily.

"Where do you want to go?" he said.

"I'll show you."

They rose from the stools. She came barely to his shoulder. He followed her quickly out of the lounge.

In the cab she talked about herself in a detached, objective way. She was an orphan. Her mother had been a show girl and her father a dude, or at least that was what the social worker at the Foundling Hospital had told her.

She had been raised in foster homes from the time she was four years old. At sixteen she had gotten a job and had been on her own, living in countless furnished rooms around the city.

At the last foster home she had learned she had a brother some five years older than herself. She had gone to the Foundling Home and they confirmed this, informing her that her brother had joined the navy when he was seventeen. More than that they could not tell her.

So she had taken to hanging around the bars and cocktail lounges frequented by navy men in the hope that some of them knew her brother.

"Have you been in the navy long?" she asked Steve suddenly.

Her hand clasped his and her body stiffened.

"Seven years," Steve said, quietly.

It was a lousy trick stringing her along like this.

"You must know a lot of navy men," she said, pleadingly.

"Hundreds," he said, shortly.

He felt guilty leading her on. It had been four long years since he'd had any real contact with the navy and he hadn't kept in touch with anyone.

"Did you ever meet a boy named Jim Powell?"

She fixed her large eyes on him pleadingly.

Steve squirmed. He pretended to reflect.

"No," he said, after what he considered a decent lapse of time. "Don't remember meeting a Jim Powell."

The tenseness went from her as suddenly as it had come. She giggled foolishly and kissed him on the cheek.

"Oh," she said, indifferently. "It doesn't matter."

They went to one of those small, anonymous hotels that flourish in the west seventies where no one is ever asked embarrassing questions about marital status or baggage and where the only requirement is that the room be paid for in advance.

Steve saw Jerry slip into the lobby as they followed the bell-hop to the elevator. The bellhop made the unnecessary trip to the room with them, unlocked the door, adjusted the steam and handed the key to Steve. He tipped the boy and closed the door behind him without locking it.

Rusty stood close to him, her blue eyes alive with excitement. Her pale skin looked cool and desirable. Her red hair was glistening with rain. She kissed him and she smelled of fresh winter rain and cheap perfume.

"Let's look around," she said. "I love to explore hotel rooms."

Steve wondered just how many hotel rooms she had explored before.

They searched the room together, testing the big, old bed with its sagging mattress and peering into the empty drawers of the large bureau. The drawers were dusty and lined with old newspapers and the bobbypins of vanished occupants.

The bathroom had large new fixtures and a new bathtub. They hung their wet coats neatly on two of the black metal hangers in the empty closet.

It was a new role for him to be calculating and cold to a pretty young girl. There were just two more steps she must take to complete the case against her and then he would have to identify himself.

"I just love hotel rooms," she said, settling down on the large, soft bed. "Don't you?"

"Yes," Steve said, dryly. "Nothing like a hotel room."

He sat stiffly in a chair facing her.

Suddenly she jumped up and began to dance gleefully about the room.

As suddenly as she had begun to dance she stopped.

"Twenty dollars," she said, pirouetting over to where he was seated.

"For the dance?" he teased.

She brushed her lips against his forehead. "For the dance, darling," she said, archly, "and other accommodations."

He gave her the money. She curtsied and placed the money in her pocketbook. Swiftly she flitted about the room turning the lights off till only one dim light was visible next to the door. She then went to the center of the room and undressed unselfconsciously before him. Her body was perfect in the imperfect light.

Steve rose self-consciously from the chair and switched on the main light.

"Police," he said, flatly, flashing his shield. "Get your clothes on. You're under arrest."

The speech sounded corny and melodramatic but it was the best he could do.

She stood perfectly still, naked in the center of the room. Her face, caught in a smile of disbelief, lost its color and blanched white.

"Oh, no," she whispered. "Not a cop."

Steve lifted her clothes from the bed and tossed them to her. "Put your clothes on," he rasped.

"But why me?" she protested. "I never did anything to you."

"Get dressed."

"Can I dress in the bathroom?" she said.

She was stalling.

"You undressed right here. I saw you. You can get dressed here," he said, grimly.

She started to dress, not looking at him. There were no tears, no recriminations. Just dead silence.

Then the door burst open. It was Jerry. He glanced casually at the girl as though it were the most normal thing in the world to open a door and walk into a room where a naked girl stood in the center of the floor.

"Hello, beautiful," he said, grinning. Then to Steve. "How's it going?"

"All right," Steve said, shortly. "She's in."

"Good," Jerry said. "The sheet's covered for the night. Make the Chief real happy."

The arrest quota sheet, Steve reflected grimly, that annoying specter that haunted every plain-clothesman. Well, he'd added another sad statistic to it.

Steve went to the closet for their coats.

Outside the rain had stopped and the night had grown old but the white and orange glow of the street lamps still dominated the city. Night people with their shut, hard faces passed them silently.

They got into Jerry's car.

"Where do you live?" Steve said to the silent girl seated between them.

She mumbled an address, keeping her eyes tightly closed and her head pressed against the back of the seat.

She lived at an address close by the docks. They stopped in front of one of two old red brick houses among the warehouses.

She lived in a small apartment on the second floor. The chairs and floor were littered with crumpled stockings and undercloth- ing. A plate, gummed with food, and a single glass stood on the table, along with an uncapped bottle of rye whisky.

"Anyone live here with you?" Steve asked.

"No," she said, not looking at him.

"Have you any relatives or friends in the city?"

She shook her head. Her large blue eyes pleaded with him.

"Can't you let me go?" she asked. She reached into her pock- etbook. "Here's your money," she said, handing him the twenty dollars he had given her.

Steve placed the money in his pocket. He didn't want to but he felt sorry for her.

"Have you anything to prove you live here?" he said brusquely.

She went to a battered dresser and removed several rent receipts from the top drawer. She handed them to him without a word. Steve studied them. Her name was Nona Powell. These would be sufficient proof of identity and the fact that she lived here. He pocketed the receipts.

"All right," he said, at last. "Let's go."

The station house was a square brick and limestone building that dominated a quiet neighborhood of private houses. The only outward sign that life was still awake somewhere inside were the twin green lights that shone over the entrance.

They opened the heavy door and went in, hurrying the reluctant girl between them. Inside, the station house smelled and sounded like a zoo with its odors and noises of confined people and their keepers. Black shades were drawn behind barred windows and dim light filtered through the long corridors.

A platoon of uniformed men was standing at parade rest on the red tiles before the high desk.

A bald-headed, solemn-faced lieutenant stood behind the desk reading off names, posts and meal times. Each man answered with a low grunt as his name was called. The men were restive, anxious to be out on the street away from the pressure of discipline.

The lieutenant glanced up sourly as Steve, Jerry and Rusty burst into the muster room.

"Who are you guys?" he barked.

"Headquarters men," Jerry said, showing his shield.

The lieutenant's voice rose in a high whine.

"Don't you guys know enough not to bust in here when I'm turning out the men?"

"Sorry, Lieutenant," Jerry said.

"What have you got?"

"A prost."

"Take her to the policewoman for search," he said, pointing to a long corridor on their left.

They hurried Rusty into a little room where a policewoman was seated at a battered desk reading a copy of *True Romance* under the naked glare of a desk lamp.

She was a big, masculine looking woman with a wide, moist face and veinous eyes.

"What do you want?" she said, dog-earing the magazine and slipping it quickly into a drawer.

"Headquarters men," Jerry explained. "Got a prost here for search."

She glared at Rusty.

What an animal, Steve thought. He glanced down at Rusty. Somehow, she seemed smaller and more unprotected than ever. Her eyes again pleaded with him. He shrugged.

"You phony sailors get out of here," the policewoman said, testily. "I'll call you when I'm through."

She took Rusty by the arm and pushed her to a green couch.

"Take everything off," she said, brusquely, folding her arms over her enormous breasts. "And no tricks."

Steve grimaced at Jerry as he closed the door quietly behind him.

"Pretty rough-looking bag," he said.

"Ain't that too bad," Jerry said.

"What she searching her for?"

"Knives, razors," Jerry said. "Anything the prost might use to hurt herself or commit suicide with."

The uniformed men filed past them and out the door into the night amidst the clump of heavy shoes and the clatter of swinging night sticks.

The court attendant, acting as Bridge man, stood on the raised platform before the bench. He was a tall, thin man with a weak face and an aquiline nose. He took his job of docket reader very seriously. He fumbled through a slender pile of onion skins. At last he motioned Steve to bring Rusty before the bench. As they stood before the bench the Bridge man sang out: "Docket Number 8-4-6, People of the State of New York versus Nona Powell, charged with Vagrancy, to wit, a common prostitute. No counsel."

Rusty stood beside Steve, facing the Magistrate. There were tight lines around her mouth, and she looked extremely pale and tired.

The magistrate, high and removed in his black robes behind the mahogany bench, spoke to Rusty in a kindly voice.

"You have the right to communicate with relatives or friends," he advised her. The speech he was making was fixed and immutable. "You are entitled to the aid of counsel at every stage of the proceedings. You have the right to an adjournment to procure counsel. Do you wish counsel?"

Rusty stared at the floor and shook her head without speaking.

"What does that mean, Miss?"

"Speak up," the rusty voice of the Bridge man instructed. "His Honor wishes to hear you."

"I'm guilty, your Honor."

The magistrate addressed Steve.

"Officer, did she give you any trouble?"

"None, your Honor."

Rusty's eyes filled with tears but she didn't cry. Here in the court, all traces of the young girl of the night before had disappeared, and it wasn't pleasant to see her.

The magistrate's massive face was thoughtful.

"How old are you, Miss Powell?"

"Twenty-two."

"Officer," the magistrate said, addressing Steve. "Was she fingerprinted?"

"Yes, sir."

"Has she any previous record?"

"None, your Honor."

Their voices echoed in the empty courtroom. The public was not admitted to the Court for Vagrant Women. The morning sun was shining bright and clear through the long, high windows of the courtroom.

The huge courtroom smelled of some kind of lemon oil that had been used to clean and polish the furniture.

"Officer, did you verify her address?"

"Yes, sir."

"What kind of work does she do?"

"She claims she is a model."

The magistrate addressed himself to the girl.

"What kind of work do you do?"

"Waitress."

Her voice was barely audible.

"You are a waitress?"

"Yes, your Honor."

The magistrate was leaning far over the bench now.

"Are you presently employed?"

"Yes, sir."

"Where?"

"At the Black Rose Restaurant on 14th Street."

"Have you ever been convicted of a crime?"

"No, sir."

"Have you ever been arrested before?"

"No."

She stared at the mahogany table in front of her.

"Look at me, please."

Rusty lifted her head and looked steadily at the magistrate. She twisted a small, white handkerchief in her right hand.

"And you wish to plead guilty to the charge preferred against you?"

"Yes."

A tall, elderly woman in uniform entered the courtroom from a door behind the bench. The magistrate turned quickly around.

"Edna," he said, addressing the elderly woman in uniform. "Has this prisoner been examined for venereal disease?"

"Yes," the elderly woman said, modestly. "She has, your Honor. She's clean."

The magistrate nodded his massive head solemnly. He adjusted his thick glasses and made notations on the papers before him.

"Miss Powell," he intoned solemnly, "I am going to accept your plea of guilty. I find you guilty as charged and I sentence you to sixty days in the Women's House of Detention."

Rusty sighed deeply and stared at the massive face unblinkingly.

The magistrate paused ponderously. At last he continued.

"However, I am going to suspend sentence and place you on probation for six months. Do you understand what that means?"

Rusty cleared her throat.

"I think so, your Honor," she said, in an unnatural, tangled voice.

"It means," the magistrate said, pointing a pontifical finger at her, "that if you are brought before this court again, at any time during your six months' probation, you will receive this sentence in addition to any other penalty which may be imposed. Is that clear?"

Rusty's slender frame trembled visibly.

"Yes, your Honor."

"Very well, Miss Powell, you are free to go."

Rusty turned abruptly and walked swiftly down the long aisle, looking neither to left nor right. In a moment the great doors swung open and shut on her hurrying form.

CHAPTER THREE

S TEVE WALKED wearily toward the two story, brown shingled building that dominated the corner of Beach Street. The old saloon was closed now, its windows boarded up and the wooden signs torn down. Alongside the house stood a gaping trench where the new thruway was being dug. Barricades and rusted flare pots stretched along the length of the trench. Soon all the houses in the area would be torn down. Many of them were already vacant. His was the only apartment still occupied in the tall old building. It was a sad, lonely place waiting for the end of things.

He had spent most of his life in the building and he had hated it. But the rent was cheap and his roots were here. The apartment he lived in was furnished exactly the way his grand-parents had left it when they had been killed in an auto accident during the war. In fact nothing had charged in this place since he had come here to live with his grandparents when his father had died. Only the people weren't here anymore. He hated everything about the place and yet he stayed. Even after the war he had returned here to live. He had never understood exactly why. He attributed it to a kind of inertia.

Steve glanced about the living room with its ancient furniture. The room smelled as always overbearingly of stale beer and liquor that permeated the boards of the building from the old saloon downstairs. For more than a century that saloon had been there. He knew that once there had existed a bright, nocturnal world. During Prohibition they had changed the face of the building, making it small and respectable looking with a real estate office in front. But the old saloon had merely been refurbished and changed into a speakeasy.

Once, when Steve was ten years old, his grandfather, who had been a night bartender in the speakeasy, had shown him the place. They had slipped through the hidden door behind the innocuous real estate office, gone along a dark, carpeted hallway until his grandfather had tapped on a door. A slit of light showed high above, a gelatinous night eye glanced down at them, and, after a moment, the door buzzed open.

The world he saw through the subdued glare of vari-colored lights was strange and unreal, without the slightest resemblance to any place he had ever seen before. Suddenly, inexplicably, his childhood had stopped and disappeared with the sudden, magical reality of a dream.

The walls and ceiling of the room were covered with huge mirrors which reflected the low light. The wide-bladed fans turned silently and lazily overhead, moving the fetid air about the room. The floor was crammed with round, blue tables and small blue leather-covered chairs. Along the full length of one wall ran a long bar made of some gleaming wood.

Steve remembered himself standing in that old room, wide-eyed and silent with wonder. And he remembered countless other times when he had sat in a corner munching pretzels and drinking ginger ale while racketeers and politicians drank and danced with their fast girls to the ragtime music of a brittle little piano played by a man who as usual was always more drunk than sober and who chain-smoked cigarettes.

A wry grin crossed Steve's face as he walked into the small living room, and absently studied the oil painting of his grandfather that hung over the imitation marble fireplace. The colors were strong and rich against the shadows of the room. A speak-easy patron had painted it many years ago.

It didn't look much like his grandfather. The beetling gray brows and deep lines in the corners of the eyes lent to them a false warmth and brightness. The artist had planned the features so cunningly they made the face seem kind and understanding.

His grandfather had been neither kind nor understanding. He had been a stern, hating, pig-headed old man who lived in a narrow little world of his own making. If, at seventy-two, he hadn't insisted on driving a car, despite a bad heart, both he and Steve's grandmother might still be alive.

Steve remembered how his grandfather had always referred to his father as "That no-good bum." He remembered his impo-tent rage at the words and his grandfather's stern insistence on his understanding how worthless his father had been. His mother had died when he was born.

Even now Steve could remember his grandfather with his corncob pipe in one corner of his mouth and the strong, acrid odor of raw-cut tobacco the old man always brought into a room with him. His childhood had been spent in hate of his grand-parents, and he had felt a long time ago that he could never love them or anyone else.

He walked quickly into the bedroom, took off his over-coat and hung it in the bedroom closet. He went out into the grubby kitchen, made coffee and poured himself a cup, drinking it black. He stared moodily at the bright sunlight. After a second cup of coffee he showered and went to bed. He felt irritated, and depressed.

As he lay in bed he seemed still to see Rusty standing naked in the hotel room. It would have been so easy to have had her. No one would have ever known. It would have been only another sordid memory. But he hadn't taken her. He had arrested her and now she was a convicted prostitute.

He rubbed his forehead tiredly. The hell with it. He had merely been doing his job and that was all. And still he saw her large blue eyes and milk-white skin and bright red hair. She dangled before him.

No girl had ever gotten under his skin before. Maybe these were only guilt feelings working on him. He wondered how he was going to stand this detail if one prostitution arrest made him feel like this. At last he turned to the wall and fell into a troubled sleep. The sunlight slowly faded from the room as shadows deepened into darkness and night.

Suddenly the wind came hurling itself from the sea, a cruel, cold wind that beat the sea against the land. The land was barren and empty. She was standing alone by the seawall. He spoke to her but she didn't hear him.

At last she turned and spoke. "I'm lost." she said. "Please help me."

He laughed. "Too bad," he said. "Everybody is lost."

He began to awaken and then

"Afraid, Steve?" Paul was chiding, his round face crinkling with amusement. "I was afraid the first time, too," he said.

Why he must have been sixteen. Paul had brought him to this house he knew down near Harlem. He didn't tell Paul. He wasn't afraid—but he didn't go in. The house was an old tenement. His Aunt Ida lived only a block from it and she was kind and good. And now his aunt was dead and a block away white and Negro prostitutes were squirming through their carnal lives. He didn't go in with Paul then, and he never went back with him to that house.

With continued fluidness scenes flowed, shifted and settled into innumerable, luminous patterns.

Somewhere, far off, a police siren sounded.

He was a small boy kneeling on a yellowed wicker seat of an "L" train and staring solemnly at houses all leaning together, at the wet looking streets as they tumbled out of view. He was wondering why the trains didn't go hurtling from the tracks to the street below.

The severe looking, gray haired woman, whose veined hand raised to strike him was his grandmother. She was warning him about something as he cowered before her. She struck him sharply across the cheek.

A young red haired girl was placing her hand lightly on his arm.

"Why are you arresting me?"

"Because you are a prostitute."

"I'm young and pretty and only wanted you to love me. You seemed so lonely."

"You're a prostitute. You're going to jail."

"I never did anything to you. Why are you arresting me?"

Suddenly he was awake again, sitting up in his bed.

CHAPTER FOUR

"STEVE," Jerry was saying, "you know the trouble with you?"

Steve stifled a wave of resentment.

"The trouble is," Jerry went on blandly, "you're too soft for this kind of work."

Steve studied Jerry's face. That slender nose would easily break under a good straight left.

"That girl the other night. The way you acted you'd think we committed a crime in arresting her."

"Drop it, will you, Jerry?"

"You're not cut out for this work," Jerry went on implacably. "How did you ever get into police work in the first place?"

Steve stiffened.

Jerry laughed and nudged Steve's arm.

"Hey, take it easy. I'm your partner."

How did I become a cop, Steve mused. Four years ago he had gone with Dan Morris to the Civil Service Commission, to keep Dan company. At the last minute Dan had talked him into filing an application. It was a spur of the moment decision. The test came and Dan flunked; Steve passed on the top of the list.

At that time he had a job doing clerical work for an oil company—rigid hours and no future and a ladder of promotion overcrowded with friends and relatives of the company executives.

When they reached his number on the police list he had wanted to go and he had. But no one at the Police Academy or elsewhere had asked him if he was emotionally and temperamentally qualified for police work and he had never questioned himself. He had passed high on the intelligence test and that was enough for him.

Steve sipped the stale beer and glanced at the red, white and blue clock over the entrance to the bar. The clock advertised the stale beer they were drinking.

"Steve," Jerry said, "did you ever know any bookies when you was a kid?"

"Not that I remember," Steve said, shaking his head.

"Well, I did. They used to take my old man for plenty, and my old man was only a garbage collector."

He looked at Steve quickly. The soft brown eyes were wary, looking for any flicker of contempt or amusement. There was none.

"A bunch of wise guys," Jerry confided, putting all his fury into the words.

Steve nodded seriously. He was fighting an impulse to laugh, but he got control of himself by thinking, "His old man was a garbage collector and mine was a bum. Swell."

"I remember when I was a kid," Jerry went on. "How those guys used to drive up in their big Caddys, with their babes. Beautiful girls! They would go to a bar and throw hundred dollar bills around just like they was quarters. And clothes! Jesus, you should have seen how those guys used to dress—like millionaires. These books today are pikers compared to those boys like my old man was supporting."

"I know what you mean," Steve said, seriously. He was consciously talking on Jerry's level. "My grandfather was a bartender in a speak. I used to see them with their fancy women."

"Yeah," Jerry continued, nodding his head in assent. "And I know how these books operate. I tell you, Steve, I know them.

Don't kid yourself I don't. I was brought up with them. I know how they think. You know what they think about cops?"

"No," Steve said.

He found it difficult to take Jerry seriously. He was always angry about something.

"They think they can buy any cop, body and soul, for a few bucks."

"Not this cop," Steve said.

"You should hear them brag how they take care of cops and nobody can hurt them. Boy, it used to make my blood boil. And now I can do something about it at last."

Was Jerry sounding him out?

"Any book I get goes and I'll convict him in court if I can," Steve said.

Just like you convicted Rusty, he thought. Jerry was right on that score. Somehow, he did feel he had committed a crime in arresting her.

Then he knew he wanted to see her again. He had her address and he knew where she worked. Then what? Then he would get to know her, explain how it was his first prostitution pinch and try to make it up to her somehow.

Steve glanced at his wristwatch. "It's ten-thirty now," he said. "Think your stoolie will show?"

Jerry grinned his tight, sly grin. "He'll show," he said with assurance. "Benny always needs money." Then Jerry nudged him. "That's him," he whispered.

Steve glanced toward the doorway and saw a figure, hardly bigger than a boy, come into the bar and shuffle through the length of the barroom toward them. As he came to the row of booths he hesitated; his back to the wall, he scrutinized the room with small, hostile eyes. When he saw Jerry, his dwarfed body grew rigid and his one good hand stiffened like a claw. The one side of his body was shrivelled and twisted and his bad hand hung useless at his side.

He was wearing a thin topcoat and a checkered cap. His face was small and pointed. And there were shadowed hollows under his pinched eyes.

Jerry nodded to him. The man slipped his bad hand into his coat pocket and shuffled, pigeon-toed, to the booth.

"Steve, meet Benny the Jockey."

They shook hands briefly. The little man's hand was tough and calloused and surprisingly strong.

"Benny here used to be one of the best jockeys in the country," Jerry said. "That was about ten years ago, wasn't it, Benny?"

"Yeah," Benny growled.

His voice was dry and listless.

"Then Benny had a little accident and things ain't been too good for him. Right, Benny?"

The little man nodded, shifting his hostile glance around the room. "I ain't got all day. I gotta get out of here," he murmured, stirring nervously on the bench.

"Sure, Benny," Jerry pacified. "Just tell us what you got."

"Double sawbuck," Benny said, holding out his clawlike hand.

"That's a lot of money," Jerry chided. "Tell us what you got."

Steve glared angrily at Jerry. He didn't like him badgering this guy. He reached into his pocket for his wallet.

Jerry reached across the table and gripped his shoulder.

"What the hell are you doing?" he whispered, angrily.

"I'm going to pay him."

"He's my stoolie. If he gets paid, I pay him. He ain't given us a thing yet."

Benny made a motion to rise and leave.

"You guys better get together," he said. "I ain't going to give nothing to two guys who can't get along with each other."

"Keep your stinking nose out of this, Benny," Jerry whispered, harshly. He slipped two ten dollar bills into the claw. "Now give us what you got and you can get the hell out of here."

Benny hesitated. His greedy eyes glanced from Jerry's face to the green flash of folding money. At last the claw closed on the money, and it was in his pocket in an instant. He glanced around the room quickly and began to talk in a nervous staccato.

"Joe the Greek opened a new wireroom back of the Community Supermarket. You know where it is?"

"Yeah, sure," Jerry said. "That new place on the boulevard."

"Right," Benny said, quickly. "Ain't very big. He got three phones and five stooges working."

"Hey," Jerry protested. "That all you got? That info ain't worth twenty bucks."

The small, hostile eyes studied Jerry.

"You ain't kidding me," the little man said, hoarsely. "It's a wireroom, ain't it." The gaunt face went tight.

"Okay, Benny, all right," Jerry quickly agreed.

The look of desperation on Benny's face had penetrated even his thick defenses.

"You got five, maybe six pinches," Benny said, quickly. "Give it to the newspapers. Have them take your pictures. They'll make regular heroes out of you guys."

Jerry and Steve laughed spontaneously.

The little man stared questioningly at Steve.

"Ain't seen you around before."

"He's my new partner," Jerry said. "Bill Murphy was dropped last week."

"Didn't get your name," Benny persisted.

"Hochuli," Steve said, slowly. "Steve Hochuli."

"See you guys around," Benny said, rising abruptly. He scrutinized the booths and bar again. They watched him shuffle cautiously through the door.

"Steve," Jerry said, excitedly. "Do you know who Joe the Greek is?"

"No," Steve said.

"His real name is Joseph Murat. He's a known gambler. Got a record as long as your arm. He's in everything from fixing races to pushing narcotics. The Chief has been after him for months. If we get him, Stevie, we'll get top pay."

Jerry's intenseness was contagious. For the first time Steve began to understand Jerry's drive to make arrests. It was a game really. It helped Jerry to rid himself of some stored up hatred. And Jerry understood the rules of this game—knew exactly what he was doing and just where he was going. Jerry's definiteness was something he couldn't help but respect.

"Pretty good little stoolie I got there, eh, Steve?" Jerry gloated.

"He gives me the creeps."

"Me, too," Jerry laughed.

They drove to within a block of the supermarket. Jerry dropped Steve off at the corner around from the parking lot behind the market.

"You walk into the lot," Jerry directed. "Hide in a doorway or something. When you see me get out of the car come right in behind me. Understand?"

"Right," Steve said.

"And keep your eyes open for a big blue Caddy. That'll be the Greek."

Steve walked slowly toward the parking lot. He stopped at a candy store and bought a newspaper.

The Community Supermarket was a spanking new raw brick structure with huge neon signs and a solid plateglass front. It was isolated from the other buildings by a half acre of gray pebbled parking lot.

He spotted Jerry's car parked in a spot directly in front of the loading platform. Jerry was slouched down in the seat with his head thrown back and his eyes closed, pretending sleep. The great metal doors of the loading platform were swung open and inside he could see sprawling piles of brown cartons and raw pine crates of oranges and apples and green winter lettuce.

He climbed into an empty truck at the far end of the lot and pretended to read his newspaper. Behind a small, barred window above the loading platform he could see a man surveying the lot. The lookout, he thought. Hadn't spotted either of them, obviously, because in the room shadowy figures still rushed back and forth.

As he watched, a pale blue Cadillac pulled up abruptly to the loading platform and a thick-set, swarthy man emerged. He was a gorilla, expensively dressed in pearl gray from his huge hat right down to his gray suede shoes—but a gorilla. The man glanced quickly over the parking lot and then darted with tremendous energy up the stairs to the loading platform and into the darkness of the storage room.

Jerry was out of the car now running to the loading platform. Steve glanced up to the barred window. The lookout was gone. He raced across the lot and was right on Jerry's heels when they were stopped by a towering, beefy-faced man wearing a pork-pie hat and a blood-stained butcher's apron.

"Where you guys think you're going?"

"Got a message for Joe the Greek," Jerry said, breathlessly.

The big man looked at them suspiciously, his little eyes studying them, trying to size them up, figure out who they were. "Yeah?" he said, questioningly.

"Yeah," Jerry said, brushing past him. "Got a message for him. Come on, Steve."

They brushed past him as the big man stared after them, puzzled.

They dashed up a short flight of wooden stairs to the room above the loading platform. Jerry put his finger to his lips in a signal for silence. They stood outside and listened. Inside the room the phones kept up a constant chatter of rings. There were hushed, secret conversations and the words were muffled.

"Can't make out a word," Jerry said. "Let's go." He opened the door to the room slowly.

A perfect tableau greeted them. All movement froze and all eyes watched as they stepped into the room. It was a moment as fragile as glass. The phones rang on but nobody answered them. Just as Benny had said, there were three phones on a table to one side of the room. The table was piled with pencils and tally sheets, scratch pads, a black record book, two piles of slips and several *National Programs*, together with copies of the *Morning Telegraph*. A small radio blared out racing results. The Greek, who had been checking the tally sheets, stared at them, sheet in hand.

"Who are you guys?" he said, hoarsely.

"Come over here," Jerry said.

The Greek lumbered to them suspiciously.

"What do you want? Is this a heist?"

"Police," Jerry said, flashing his shield.

"Hell," the Greek said, working up a smile. "Why didn't you say so in the first place. I thought it was a heist."

Steve walked quickly over to the table.

"Everybody stand up," he said, quietly. "Don't move your hands and get against that wall."

"Hey," the Greek shouted excitedly. "What the hell's the matter with that guy."

He ran to Steve, grabbing at his shoulder. Steve spun easily around, took a firm hold on the collar of the Greek's natty coat and threw him against the wall.

"Stay there and keep quiet," he commanded.

"All right," Jerry said, joining Steve. "Everybody turn to the wall and keep your hands out of your pockets."

The six men turned to the wall in unison.

"Place your hands against the wall above your heads."

The men obeyed silently.

The telephones kept up a noisy racket.

Joe the Greek's short arms moved slightly. In a flash Steve was on him. The Greek's hairy fist shot upward to Steve's jaw, but the blow slipped harmlessly past Steve's ear. In a single motion he cracked a short, hard left hand to the swarthy jaw and spun the Greek around hard so that his head banged solidly against the wall.

Jerry had his gun out.

"Nobody make a move," he shouted. "Frisk him, Steve."

Steve quickly ran his hands along the Greek's barrel-like chest. He felt the bulk of a gun under the man's left armpit. Deftly he slipped the gun from its holster. It was a short-barreled, blunt nosed Colt Cobra. A nasty toy. He found a second small automatic hidden in the Greek's soft felt hat.

"This guy's a walking arsenal," he called to Jerry.

"Keep going," Jerry said. "See if he has any tickets on him. We'll really wrap this baby up."

Steve found a dozen racing slips and payoff sheets in the Greek's inside jacket pocket.

"Please, you guys," the Greek pleaded, hoarsely, his words bouncing off the wall in front of him.

"Yeah?" Jerry said.

"Can I talk?"

"Sure, go ahead and talk."

"I'll go for a big one," the Greek said.

"What does that mean?"

"A thousand bucks if you forget the whole thing," the Greek propositioned, his face turning away from the wall trying to see their expressions.

Jerry and Steve laughed grimly.

"Two grand, you guys. I'll go for two grand."

"Shut up, Joe," Steve said flatly. "Save your money for the lawyers, the bondsmen and the court."

The Greek attempted to turn around again. Steve pushed the dark head, and the man's forehead snapped sharply against the wall.

"Stay put," Steve said, softly.

"You guys must be crazy," the Greek protested bitterly.

"Sure," Steve said. "We're crazy."

Jerry was already on the phone calling for the police wagon.

They gathered all the evidence and bundled it into two large paper bags. Jerry disconnected the three phones. They went into the bags along with the other evidence.

"Hey," one of the men called. "Can we take our hands down now? We're getting tired."

"Sure," Steve said. "Only no false moves or somebody will get hurt."

The Greek's beady eyes followed Steve's every move. He mumbled something under his breath.

"What did you say?"

"I'm going to get you," the Greek whispered, his eyes dilated and hard as agate.

"You do that," Steve said, laughing easily. "After you get out of jail."

They heard the heavy clatter of feet on the steps outside and in a moment three uniformed patrolmen were in the room to take the prisoners away.

Sculptured in the flood of bright winter sunlight the shabby old neighborhood of tenements and crumbling shops looked momentarily clean and young again.

Steve and Jerry circled the area in the car and parked a short distance from the Taxicab Feed Line and the candy store Goldie used as a numbers drop. Goldie was a notorious numbers collector who had been working this depressed area for almost a quarter of a century. He had been arrested only once.

As they watched they saw a fat man with a bloated night-face waddle out of the shadows into the sunlight and toward the taxicab drivers who were huddled near their cabs.

Goldie squinted myopically up and down the street. After a brief conversation with the cabbies he accepted money from them and made notations on a white slip of paper which he held cupped in his hand.

"Let's go," Steve said, excitedly. "He's taking action right on the street."

Jerry slipped from the car and walked rapidly toward the candy store into which Goldie had gone after collecting from the cabbies. Steve followed close behind.

From their vantage point in a hallway they saw Goldie enter a telephone booth in the little store.

"Let's get him," Jerry whispered.

They hurried across the street and into the store.

Goldie squinted at them myopically from the phone booth and stuffed a slip of paper into his mouth, chewing on it and swallowing hard.

"Get him, Steve," Jerry shouted. "He's swallowing the work."

He pulled the man from the booth but it was too late. Goldie gulped and gave a self-satisfied grin.

"Hello, boys," he said, mildly.

"Beat us again, eh, Goldie?" Jerry said, giving the man a quick but thorough frisk. "Clean. Clean as a whistle." He threw up his hands in disgust.

Suddenly he grabbed the little fat man by the throat.

"Don't ever do that again, Goldie," Jerry warned in his angry, lisping voice.

Goldie gently raised his plump hands to his throat. He stroked his throat softly and sadly.

"Do you have to be so rough?" he protested feebly. "I don't know why you guys keep pestering me. I ain't collecting numbers no more. I'm working now."

"Where you working, Goldie?" Steve asked.

"I'm a jewelry salesman."

Jerry searched the telephone booth and came up with nothing. He shrugged his shoulders at Steve.

"Who you working for?"

"Myself. I work on consignment. I only sell to my friends. I could maybe get you a nice ring for your girl?" he said, smiling politely at Steve.

Jerry gave Goldie a sudden shove. "Get going," Jerry said, "Don't bull us. Get lost."

"You guys ain't got no right to do this," Goldie said, straightening his tie and glaring at them. "I'm going to report you guys."

The cunning night-face was flushed with anger.

Jerry was smiling now. "Sure," he said, "you go ahead and report us, Goldie."

Goldie lit a cigarette with trembling fat white hands and turned away from them. He waddled out of the store, his small fat frame quivering with righteous indignation.

The candy-store owner watched them closely from behind the counter.

"You better keep the numbers boys out of this joint," Jerry warned, "or we'll close you up for keeping and maintaining."

"Me?" the man said, a flicker of contempt in his small, bland eyes. "This store is public. I can't stop nobody from coming in here."

Jerry surveyed the skimpy stock of uncovered chocolate candy, the few packs of cigarettes and the outdated, dusty magazines.

"You ain't kidding us," he said. "You ain't making no living from this dump. You're in the numbers racket up to your ears."

The man folded his thick arms over his chest, imperturbable and silent but only for a moment.

"You think that way," he snapped, "you think I'm in the numbers business lock me up. Go ahead, lock me up right now."

"We'll get you yet, wise guy," Jerry said.

Steve stood quietly at the entrance to the store. Jerry was angry and spouting off again. Steve made it a policy never to threaten. If they got a bookie or policy man with the stuff, they made an arrest. If they didn't, they dropped their tails between their legs and beat it. Threats only put them on their guard.

But Jerry wasn't buying that.

"We'll be watching you, wise guy," he said, sauntering to the store entrance.

The man leaned over the counter pugnaciously. "Watch away," he shouted, contemptuously. "Ruin my business. But don't take no candy on the way out!"

They walked silently back to the car. Suddenly Jerry gripped Steve's arm. "Look at that," he said, staring at a sleek blue Cadillac.

It was Joe the Greek driving with a canary yellow blonde snuggling up to him in the seat. They were talking and laughing animatedly.

"Not a care in the world," Steve said, shaking his head in wonder. It was only a week since the Greek had been arraigned on the gun and gambling charges. He was out on two thousand dollars bail, but it didn't seem to worry him much. The case would probably drag through the courts for more than a year before it was concluded one way or the other.

"Wow," Jerry said. "What a number she was!"

"Want to follow them?" Steve suggested.

Jerry vetoed the idea. "He would only ride us all over town. It's hard to tail a guy in the daytime unless you use a couple of cars."

They got in Jerry's car and drove aimlessly around the area. Everything was quiet. It was bookmaking and policy time, but there didn't seem to be anything doing in this part of town. The sheet wasn't covered and they had no leads. They both felt uncomfortably tense.

"Boy, could we use some information this month," Jerry said, expressing Steve's thought.

Steve nodded.

They drove down a side street to a towering apartment house that blocked off the sun and shadowed the street.

"Ed and Bill have a wiretap going in there," Jerry said as he parked the car.

They walked cautiously down a narrow flight of cement steps into the dimly lit basement. Steve followed Jerry's tall, loose-limbed figure through the dusty, winding passageways. The foul air smelled of coal gas and dampness. Jerry tapped on a door that led to a storage room.

Ed Manely opened the door. He was a young, heavy-set man in coveralls and a cap. He looked more like a butcher boy than a member of the Vice Squad.

"Hi, Ed," Jerry said, cheerfully, "how's the tap coming?"

A tiny night light was on in the room, and it made every-thing seem murky and fluid like objects seen under water. They followed Ed toward a far corner of the windowless room.

"Watch that baby-carriage," Ed warned, walking around it. The room was cluttered with old washing machines, refrigerators and carriages and sleighs.

As their eyes became accustomed to the semidarkness they made out Bill Wyman's stumpy figure crouched in a corner. He was seated on a child's sleigh, smoking quietly. An earphone was clamped to his head. At his feet was a box that looked like a por-table phonograph. The earphone was hooked to the box. On one side of the box was a phonograph record set on a tiny turntable. The record wasn't moving.

"Pull up a sleigh and sit," Ed whispered, grinning.

"Got anything?" Steve asked.

"Not yet. The dame's been getting calls all morning. All they say is, 'Hello, Madam,' and then she gives them telephone num-bers to call. I can't figure out if she's running a call girl service or working for a book."

"Can she hear us talking?" Steve said.

"She can't hear us," Bill said.

"Anybody know you're here?" Jerry said.

"Just the super. Nice guy. Brought us coffee a few minutes ago. We got him bulled we're the F.B.I."

"What's this thing hooked up to?" Steve said.

"We got it back-strapped from the box outside."

Bill looked at Steve quizzically.

"Ever work with wiretaps?" he asked.

"No."

"We'll have to teach you one of these days," Bill said, vaguely. "Know what a backstrap is?"

"No."

Bill was pleased to display his knowledge.

"It's just an extension wire. We didn't want to work outside where the tenants might see us so we hooked a wire to the box and brought it in here."

Suddenly Bill clamped his hand against the earphone and signaled for silence. In a moment he reached over and switched on the record. The tiny record began to spin silently round and round recording the conversation.

"Her boy friend," Bill explained. "Name's Vic. He's making a date. The Washington Bar at five tonight. She'll meet him. Her husband's working late tonight."

Suddenly he shook his head from side to side, his broad mouth open in amazement. "Wow, the things this guy says to her."

"Been here long?" Jerry said.

"Since seven this morning."

"Got anything we can help on?"

"Only these numbers. We'll let you know after we check them out."

Steve wished he could get out of the cellar. He didn't like prying into people's private lives, not this way.

Bill stretched his stumpy legs and leaned back against the wall.

"Gone dead now. May be a stiff for the rest of the day."

"Tough," Jerry said, rising and yawning. "Won't let us in on it, eh?"

"It's not that, Jerry," Bill said, quickly. "We haven't got anything, yet."

"No, eh?" Jerry said, his voice filled with disbelief.

"Don't be that way," Bill said.

"Let's go, Steve," Jerry said, ignoring him.

Leaving the basement was like coming up from deep, dirty water. Back there he had felt as though he were drowning and his feelings had been submerged in the dark murkiness of basements and wiretaps. As they emerged once more into the bright light his thoughts brightened.

"Let's call it a day, Jerry," he said, hesitating at the corner.

He wanted to be rid of him and Jerry knew it.

"Okay with me," Jerry said, neutrally. "Day's a stiff anyway." But his face broke into a knowing grin and the brown eyes were mocking. "I'll sign you out at the office."

"Thanks," Steve said, getting into his car.

If he hurried he might catch Rusty at the shop.

CHAPTER FIVE

STEVE SLAMMED the car into gear and turned off the bumpy cobblestones to follow the smooth trolley tracks underneath the elevated. A train crashed overhead sending a blue stream of sparks down. He turned the wheel expertly and headed the car toward the bridge that speared across the river.

The Black Rose Restaurant was one of those small, obscure restaurants that haunt the shopping area along 14th Street. Day workers and shoppers had already gone home and the evening crowds had not yet entered the area. The place was almost empty when he entered.

He found a table in the rear. The air was spicy with the smells of food from the kitchen. A waiter in a black alpaca coat and bow tie came over to the table, pulling out his pencil and order pad.

"What's yours?"

"Where's Rusty?" Steve said, briefly.

The waiter smiled knowingly. He pointed to the kitchen.

"Tell her a friend of hers is here."

"She's got lots of friends," the waiter said, winking suggestively. "What's your name?"

"Just tell her there's a guy wants to see her," Steve said, sharply.

"Yes, sir! Yes, sir!" the waiter said, backing away in mock fear at Steve's anger.

The waiter went into the kitchen and in a moment Rusty came out looking more desirable than ever in a tight pink uniform with a tiny apron, and a bit of laced cap perched on her piled-up red hair. She was smiling her twisted, open-city smile. She recognized him instantly, and her eyes filled with panic. She hesitated as though she wanted to run and then, somehow, she gained control of her fear. In an automatic gesture she drew a pencil and order pad from her apron and approached his table.

"Hello, Rusty," he said, smiling at her.

"What are you doing here?"

Her voice was frozen and her deep-scooped lips were pursed in lines of disapproval and fear.

"I came to see you."

"Why?"

I wish I knew, he thought. "No reason," he finally blurted out.

"Is it part of your job to come here?"

"No," he said quietly, lighting a cigarette and blowing the smoke ceilingward.

"Look," she said, her blue eyes filling with tears. "Won't you please get out of here? Do you want me to lose my job?"

"Nobody knows I'm a cop," he said.

"That's what you think," she said. "You look and act like a cop. You even smell like a cop."

"Take it easy," he said, attempting to take her hand, but she drew quickly away from him. She stiffened and that piquant cast was back in her eyes. She tapped her pencil nervously against the order pad and refused to meet his gaze.

"All right," he said.

"I'm not under arrest now, am I?"

"No." He shook his head slowly. "You're not under arrest."

"Then just give me your order."

He ordered a sandwich and coffee. The waiter in the black alpaca coat and bow tie delivered the order and dropped the bill in his lap.

"Pay on the way out," the waiter said, flatly.

Steve felt strangely humiliated. He watched Rusty as she waited on the other tables. She ignored him completely. At last he finished his sandwich and coffee, paid his check and left. He didn't leave a tip.

He headed the car uptown. He was seated in his car watching when Tommy Gozzi jockeyed his cab into the last position on the feed line. Tommy was a bookmaker who worked nights and reputedly took bets from the other cab drivers. So far he hadn't been spotted. He might get a line on Tommy's operation tonight. It was early and he felt too restless to go home.

He watched Tommy as he left his cab and headed for the steam-grimed window of the all-night diner. The cabbies were all there, arguing and drinking coffee and eating buns and dough-nuts. Tommy bought a copy of *The Star* at the all-night candy store and went into the diner.

Steve left the car and sauntered to the diner, peering in through the window. The grime and steam obscured his view. Tommy didn't know him. He would take a chance on going inside.

When he entered the diner the counterman gave a low, sharp whistle and the place went dead. Nobody looked in his direction but he knew that whistle was the signal that he had been spotted as a cop. He ordered coffee, drank it quickly and left. Tonight just wasn't his night.

He went into a late movie uptown but the place was crowded. After standing for forty-five minutes looking at a dull western he gave up and went home.

He tried to study the material for the Sergeant's Test but he couldn't concentrate. Suddenly he couldn't stand it any more.

Tonight he wanted to go out somewhere and forget the fool he made of himself.

On an impulse he called Helen Kilbride. He had known Helen a long time, but she unashamedly wanted to marry and Steve didn't intend marrying anyone for a long, long time.

Helen's voice over the phone was low and sweet. No, she didn't have a date. No, it wasn't too late. Yes, she would like to go dancing with him.

She lived far out in the suburbs on a street where all the low priced houses were carbon copies of each other and were packed close together. At the end of the street was a wooden fence holding back acres of weeds.

Standing in front of the door to her house, he hesitated. Two months ago at a houseparty Helen had almost gone all the way with him. They had both been pretty drunk. Tonight she might go all the way. He hoped so. He felt guilty because it wasn't Helen he wanted. You have a childish conscience, he thought.

They checked their coats at the cloakroom and crossed the room to a table away from the orchestra.

An old man with silver-rimmed spectacles and cheap false teeth took their order.

"Let's dance," Steve said, as the orchestra struck into a sleepy melody.

"Not yet," Helen said, self-consciously. "Wait till some others are on the floor."

The waiter brought them their drinks and they drank without talking. It was as though some desperate contest were going on between them.

Suddenly the dance floor was crowded with couples. The orchestra was playing a slow waltz. It was Steve's kind of music. "Now?" he said.

Helen rose smiling. She followed his awkward steps easily. He felt the soft, slender lines of her body, warm and supple against him. Her face was cool and her skin smelled of perfume and health. The dance ended and they returned to their table. He signaled the hovering waiter and ordered more drinks.

"How are things going in the Police Department?" Helen said finally.

"Pretty well," he said. "I'm on the Vice Squad now."

"Why, that's wonderful," she said. "Do you like it?"

"Sometimes," he said.

"You don't seem very happy." She placed her hand on his. "Is something wrong, Steve?"

"No," he lied.

The little waiter was buzzing around them again, really pushing the drinks.

"Anything else for you folks?"

They ordered more drinks.

The dance floor was too crowded now for dancing.

"Quite a lineup there," Steve said, nodding toward the people queued behind a velvet rope hooped to shiny brass stanchions.

"Do you want to leave, Steve?"

"Where to?" he asked and called the waiter.

Helen's dark eyes smiled at him ingenuously.

"Oh, let's just ride in the car."

"Good idea," he said and paid the bill.

Outside in his car Helen sat very close. They drove a winding highway toward the Island.

"There's a pier we can drive out on and look at the bay," Helen volunteered.

They found the pier and parked the car at the far end in the deep night shadows.

For a long time they sat in silence staring out over the silken black water and the limned, nameless shapes of light and shadow and boats bobbing up and down in the bay.

"Want to get out and stretch your legs?"

He was too restless to sit still for long.

"Let's," Helen said, opening the door and stepping out, gathering her coat close about her against the chill, salt wind.

They walked to the edge of the pier listening to the thick water piling up and lapping around the pilings and breathed deeply of the cold, tangy sea air.

She moved very close to him and he could hear her breath coming fast.

He kissed her and slipped his hand beneath her coat, pressing it softly against her small, warm breasts.

"Don't, Steve," she moaned.

"Why not?" he said, laughing and kissing her hard on the mouth.

He felt her tremble and press against him.

"Cold?"

"No."

His hands grew bolder. "What's wrong, Helen?"

"Don't make me do anything wrong, please, Steve?"

"Do you want to?"

"Yes, yes, of course, I want to very much," she moaned in a tight, tangled voice. "But I mustn't—I won't until—"

The fragile mood was shattered, and he drew away from her. A nice, clean American kid whose only wish was to marry and have a home and kids, he thought cynically. Why in hell had he ever bothered to call her?

"Let's go," he said, striding back to the car.

She got in next to him sheepishly. Her eyes were wet and her face drawn.

"For Christ's sakes, don't cry."

"I'm sorry, Steve."

"What for?" he said, bitterly. "You didn't do anything to be sorry for."

"But I wanted to. That's what's wrong."

Steve raced the motor and they drove back in silence.

Suddenly he was thinking of Rusty again. She wouldn't lead a man on that way. She would go all the way and never regret anything. And she was a two-bit whore who walked the streets and bummed around bars and didn't give a damn if she ever got married.

The waiter in the black alpaca coat and bow tie looked down his nose at Steve, a wicked grin on his face.

"She quit two days ago."

"Say where she was going?"

"No. Just quit. You want something to eat?" The waiter's eyes were filled with a malicious pleasure.

Without answering Steve rose and left the place. The waiter snickered after his retreating figure.

He drove to the Police Academy. The class was already in session and all the seats were taken. He stood quietly in back of the room and listened to the lecturer's dry voice swell and fall over the heads of the ambitious policemen who were busily taking notes. The examination was only two weeks away and he couldn't care less. At last he couldn't stand it anymore and left.

He drove aimlessly about the city trying to get Rusty out of his mind. At last it started to get dark. He stopped at a restaurant, ate a tasteless dinner and went home. He went to bed but he could not sleep. He wondered what had happened to her. Why had she quit her job? He could not get out of his mind the idea that she was in trouble.

He thought sleepily of her full lips and red hair. He wanted to kiss them and he wanted to make love to her. Again he thought of her in the hotel room. All she had offered him for twenty dollars he wanted.

He glanced at the luminous hands of the Big Ben on the night table next to the bed. Eleven-thirty. He stumbled out of bed and switched on the bedroom light. Finally, he showered, dressed and hurried from the house.

He drove among the groups of gray houses close to the waterfront. The night air was crisp and cold and smelled of the sea. At last, among the giant warehouses, he found the street and drove up from the docks to the worn brick tenement.

The hot mouth of the hallway was sticky, filled with the rank odors of bad drains and moldy wood. He climbed the stairs and stopped outside the door of her apartment. A stream of light flowed from a crack where the door did not quite reach the warped sill. He could hear a waltz tune coming from a radio somewhere inside the apartment.

He tried the door. It was unlocked. He walked in without knocking, and found her sitting in the bedroom by the window. She was dressed in the cheap gray coat and green dress with the impossibly high-heeled shoes she had been wearing the night he arrested her. On the bed was a worn valise half-filled with clothing.

Her red hair was combed into a high pompadour and she had applied a good deal of makeup to her face and eyes. There was something wrong with her eyes. They seemed smoky and far away as though she couldn't focus them.

Suddenly she seemed aware of him. She stared at him and turned her eyes away without speaking.

"Hello, Rusty," he said, trying to make his voice sound friendly and casual. "Didn't mean to frighten you."

She looked squarely at him as though seeing him for the first time, and there was deadly fear in her eyes. Then she looked at him pleadingly.

"Don't stop me," she whispered, hoarsely.

He felt her terror. "I won't stop you," he said, reassuringly.

Suddenly she laughed. The sound echoed unpleasantly in the quiet, untidy room. It was as though something inside her were out of control and she were drifting.

"I know you won't," she said. Her voice was hard and brittle.

"How do you know that?" he said, quietly.

"Because you are in love with me."

She was playing some kind of game with him, and he didn't understand it at all.

"You quit your job."

"That's none of your business," she cried out.

He glanced at the old valise on the bed.

"Moving?"

She rose and walked erratically about the room, teetering on her high heels. At last she sat down, lit a cigarette and whistled tunelessly, her eyes drifting out of focus.

"Expecting someone?"

She stared at him, hatred flaming in her eyes.

"It's been hard putting you out of my mind," he confessed. "I wish you wouldn't hate me."

She glanced at him distrustfully, with her bright, smoky eyes.

"Too bad," she said.

He watched the anger burning in her tortured face and felt a sense of acute helplessness. He couldn't control what had happened before, and he couldn't do anything about what was happening now.

There was a light tap on the apartment door.

"Come in, Tony," she called, relaxing visibly.

Tony came in—short, handsome and very dapper, stinking of smart money.

"Who's he?" Tony queried, jerking his head in Steve's direction.

"The cop that locked me up."

One of Steve's eyelids began to twitch up and down.

"You got any business here?" Tony asked, crisply. The hard brown eyes stared unblinkingly at Steve.

"You going with him?" he said to Rusty.

She laughed a little wildly and danced over to Tony, kissing him hard on the mouth, forcing her body against his.

"You get the hell out of here," Tony said in a flat, hard voice.

"Make me," Steve said, then knew he'd been stupid.

"Tony," Rusty interfered. "He's a bastard. Don't argue with him. If he won't go, we will. We know where to go."

Steve shrugged his shoulders hopelessly.

He turned without a word and left the apartment. As he walked slowly down the stairs he could hear them laughing above the music of the radio.

CHAPTER SIX

THE ROOF of the old factory building towered above the neighboring apartment dwellings. The rain had stopped and in the low, clear light of evening Steve and a man named Sid Smith looked down over the courtyards, tangled alleys and tumbled roofs of the city to the river and the tapering smoke-stacks of the factories near the water.

They were crouched beside the warm bricks of the factory chimney they were using as a shield to avoid being silhouetted against the sky.

As they watched, a heavily laden station wagon pulled into one of the alleys beside the apartment houses. Two burly men began systematically unloading large pieces of furniture from the wagon and hustling them into the basement of the house. In a few minutes a low-slung foreign car pulled up behind the station wagon, and a fleshy, prosperous looking man stepped out and spoke to the men.

"That's the bastard," Sid Smith said, nudging Steve with a bony elbow. "Last week I won ten grand in his dice game. He gives me two gorillas to escort me home. They leave me on the corner across from my house and I don't get halfway across the street when two guys with guns step out from beside my house and heist me for everything I got."

Sid Smith was a small, thin man with a sunken chest. His round grey eyes were faded and his tight-skinned face was yellow and deeply lined. He was an inveterate gambler who followed the big booked dice games from borough to borough and even to Jersey. He owned a small but lucrative jewelry business down on the Bowery.

Steve had known Sid since he was a boy because Sid had patronized the speakeasy where Steve's grandfather had worked. When Steve had gone overseas, Sid had given him an expensive gold wristwatch as a going-away gift. When he had been robbed of the ten thousand he had come to Steve with the information on Duke Silvers' game. His fury at being robbed had overcome his natural fear of anything that might happen to him if it was found out he had informed. Rumor had it that Sid had once lost as much as fifty thousand dollars in a single night at a floating crap game.

"See that furniture," Sid hissed, excitedly. "Those are the tables broken down by sections so they can cart them around in that station wagon. Duke's rented some dame's apartment in that house. Now all you have to find out is which apartment he's using."

"How does he get them to rent out their apartments?"

"Money," Sid said, simply.

Sid was studying Steve. You cops don't know nothing, his eyes said. The trouble with you cops is you never played dice or placed a bet on a horse in your lives. And they put dopes like you, young, inexperienced kids, on the Vice Squad and send you out to catch old timers; gamblers who are cute and shrewd and know all the angles. The only guys you'll catch are the dopes and the unlucky ones.

"Here's how he works," Sid said, patronizingly, gesturing with his thin, bony hands. "Duke gets some widow or young couple who needs money. He rents their apartment for a friendly card game for his friends, see?"

Steve nodded, offering Sid a cigarette.

"Don't smoke up here," Sid whispered, nervously. "They would spot us in a minute."

He was right. Steve replaced the cigarette in the pack.

"Get it?" Sid was saying. "The tenants know there's something fishy about Duke's story but the money is too much for them. They figure they're in the clear anyway, being out of the house. Once Duke has a place, he dumps their furniture into the bathroom and the closets and sets up his equipment. Then he has his boys pick up the players in cars at various pre-arranged spots throughout the city and bring them to the location."

"Neat," Steve said. "Very neat."

"Yeah," Sid said, his face breaking into a hard grin. "And it has been going on since before you was born."

"The Chief was mentioning Duke Silvers' game only the other day," Steve volunteered. "It hasn't been taken in nine months."

Sid Smith started to laugh but broke into a soft cough.

"Hey," Steve said, "look at that."

He was watching a rear apartment on the third floor. The lights were on and inside men could be seen busy dismantling the living room furniture and carrying it out of the room. Other men were assembling two large gambling tables and installing portable air conditioners in the living room windows.

"Yeah," Sid said, nodding his small head. "Now, Steve, I don't want you getting hurt. Remember, Duke has two lookouts working for him. One is Blimp Kreis. He stays downstairs on the outside as the lookout. He looks like a fat blimp and is a sharp dresser. Must hit three hundred and fifty pounds. They hook up a buzzer to the apartment bell. If the Blimp sees anything that looks like cops he steps on the buzzer and they all beat it."

"Nice setup," Steve said.

"Now listen!" Sid said seriously. "He's got another lookout who stands in the hallway. That's Stretch Golden. He's over six-five and built like a pencil."

Sid paused and pointed his bony finger impressively at Steve. "Now these two gorillas you got to watch them. First, don't let them make you. And if they do make you, have your gun ready. They look like a comedy team, but they're both armed and dangerous. The Blimp carries a gun strapped to a spring in his coat sleeve. When he drops his right hand the gun pops into it. And he knows how to use that gun."

Steve stared at the frightened little man.

"Stretch is a knife man. He has a switchblade strapped to his right leg. Don't let him get to it."

"Don't worry," Steve reassured him. "We'll get them."

"I hope you do," Sid said, vehemently. "I hope you get every one of them bums."

He scratched the back of his thin hand nervously.

"Well," he said, finally, "guess that wraps it up."

They shuffled cautiously to the door, holding their bodies in a half-crouch. Inside the building an old watchman was waiting with the elevator. He took them down. Sid slipped him a bill as he let them out the side door of the building.

As the plumbing truck pulled to a stop in front of the building Steve jumped out, pushed his cap up and looked at a slip of white paper in his hand.

"This is the place," he shouted to Jerry.

No sign of Blimp Kreis but he'd be around somewhere.

Jerry swung out of the truck and together they lugged a white toilet bowl from the back of the truck.

They wore dirty caps, coveralls with *"Jack's Plumbing Shop"* stitched conspicuously across the backs, and battered work shoes.

Steve grunted loudly as he hoisted the bowl onto his broad back. "Damn thing is heavy," he said, glancing quickly about for signs of the lookout.

In the glare of the street lights he could make out Bill Wyman's stumpy figure coming toward them. Bill was dressed neatly in a business suit and carrying a briefcase and a folded newspaper. He looked for all the world like a tired clerk coming home from a hard day at the office. From the opposite end of the street Ed Manley, in work clothes, was hurrying toward them balancing a large bag of groceries in his arms. They looked unbelievably innocent.

"Some hour to be called for a job," Jerry said, lifting a big leather bag of tools to his shoulder.

As they walked slowly up the narrow steps of the stoop, a nattily dressed billikin detached itself from the shadows of the vestibule and held the door open for them. Blimp Kreis! There was no mistaking his three hundred and fifty pounds.

"Working late, fellas?" he said in a cool, pleasant voice that sounded as though it could get real tough.

"Yeah," Steve grunted. "Emergency. Bowl split on the second floor. Water all over the place."

"Hold that door will you, Mac," Jerry said.

The Blimp held the door as they puffed through.

"Jezus, I'm dead," Jerry said, tiredly.

Steve grunted loudly as he mounted the steps. He didn't have to pretend the toilet bowl was getting heavier by the second.

They kept up a constant patter of gripes as they shuffled slowly up the steps to the third floor. On the third floor landing they unloaded the bowl and bag of tools.

Stretch Golden cat-footed down the long corridor toward them.

"Hi," he said, "what's up?"

Steve pointed his gun at the tall, pencil-shaped man's belly.

"Police," he hissed. "Freeze where you are."

Jerry quickly found the switchblade strapped to the man's right leg. He ripped it off and slipped it into his pocket.

"Face the wall. Don't move your hands or make a sound."

In a moment Blimp Kreis came puffing up the stairs prodded from behind by Bill and Ed.

"Everything okay?" Bill whispered.

"So far," Steve said. "All right, guys," he whispered to Stretch and Blimp, "lead the way."

They minced down the long corridor to the rear apartment.

"Knock and tell them to open up."

He nudged Stretch Golden with the gun. Stretch hesitated. He dug the gun deeper into the man's bony back.

Stretch knocked three times and to the muffled inquiry from inside answered, "It's me. Stretch!"

The door swung open and a blast of cool, clear air struck them. As they stepped inside they could hear the low hum of the air conditioners above the conversations in the apartment. There were the two gambling tables set up in the living room, surrounded by men. One was a trough-like affair in which the dice were bounding over the green velvet. It was being worked by a stick man. There was a dealer in the slot of the other table and a game of blackjack was in full swing. The usual assortment of well-dressed businessmen, bookmakers and racketeers were there. They all had the hypnotized look of a flashlight picture.

"Police," Bill shouted in his deep, authoritative voice. "This is a raid. Nobody make a move."

Even as he spoke, Steve could hear the shriek of the prowl car sirens as they stopped in front of the house and the tramp of heavy feet in the hallway below. The raid had been perfectly timed.

"Everybody against the wall," Steve commanded. The men slouched against the wall without speaking.

In the kitchen the refrigerator was stacked with refreshments and sandwiches. Two cases of beer were on the floor loaded with ice and on the sink were trays of glasses and bottles of whisky.

Soon they had all the players rounded up, finding them hidden under the beds and in the closets. One man was stopped as he tried to crash through a closed window onto the fire escape.

Finally more than fifty men were lined up in the living room.

Bill scooped up the piles of bills and change from the gambling cases and dumped them into the briefcase he was carrying. He gathered up several boxes of new dice and two dozen decks of cards still in their new containers.

Outside the apartment the sounds of tramping feet and nightsticks hitting the banisters could be heard and in a moment the uniformed men were marching the prisoners downstairs to the waiting patrolwagons.

The raid had gone off smooth as silk.

Duke Silvers, his fat face shiny with sweat, pleaded with them.

"Can't I talk to you guys?" he whined. "I'm a good guy. I always take care of the cops. Ask anybody."

"You're lying in your teeth, fat boy," Bill said. "For almost a year we been on your tail. We got you and you ain't getting away."

"What about the money you took from the tables?" Duke cried. "How about that? It's mine."

"Prove it ain't gambling money and you get it back. Otherwise it goes to the welfare fund."

"Hey, Whitey," Jerry called to one of the waiting uniformed men. "Take fat boy out of here."

Whitey came over quickly and hustled Duke Silvers out the door.

The plain-clothesmen set to dismantling the tables and gambling paraphernalia and brought it downstairs to be loaded into the patrolwagons. Only a few neighbors were curious enough to look out their windows to see what was happening.

After the players, stickmen, dealers, gorillas and Duke Silvers were booked at the station house and the evidence turned over to the desk officer for delivery to the property clerk, the plain-clothesmen went to a bar for a nightcap.

When Steve arrived home he felt happy for the first time since he had arrested Rusty.

Steve was in fact soon finding life generally pleasant again. Jim Rogers, one of the young plain-clothesmen, had begun dating a girl from out-of-town who lived in a furnished apartment near Columbia University. She shared the apartment with a girl friend and it was to her that Steve was invited to confine his attentions. Steve had found this easy; she turned out to be an agreeable, plain girl with a sense of humor.

Sally McDonald was about twenty-two, rather tall, with an open, scrubbed face. She had very grave eyes, good cheek-bones and a full mouth. Her skin was smooth and blond looking, her eyebrows a thin dark line and her hair, thick and yellow, drawn straight back. She came from a small town in Ohio and was taking graduate work in Sociology at Columbia.

Once she found out he'd had two years of college she razzed him unmercifully for not finishing and settling for a cop's job. He countered by imitating her twangy talk and reminding her she came from Sherwood Anderson country, where everybody quit working at forty, put on a hat and departed for parts unknown.

To Sally he was a typical New Yorker—a man who associated with racketeers, who never slept and who knew the city like the palm of his hand. He talked to her endlessly about New

York—about the racketeers who controlled the gangs and who lived in fine houses and respectable neighborhoods in the outlying suburbs; about the bookmaking and numbers rackets; the bums who prowled the streets searching for cigarette butts and handouts; the old women who crept along the city streets late at night and in the early morning, lifting lids off garbage cans and searching around inside for bits of rotten food; the degenerates who frequent the subways, cabarets and hotels; criminals, fumed with drink or drugs or half-insane with "smoke."

They went everywhere together: to the theater, to lectures and concerts and to the night courts of the city. Sally was an inexhaustable well of enthusiasm and questions. Often he attended her classes at Columbia and read books in the college library while she did research for her courses. Afterward they would stroll down the winding macadam paths that led through the terraced grounds below Riverside Drive. At night the park was deserted and the park lights were white spots pasted against the darkness. The massive buildings towering above them on the Drive looked darkly ominous and inaccessible.

It was Sally who consoled him when he failed the Sergeant's Test. They went to her apartment and drank scotch and soda until they were both quite drunk and when he tried to take off her clothes, she lifted her slender arms obediently as he slipped her dress over her head. Later he felt ashamed for her that she had turned out to be such an easy lay.

One night he took her to Coney Island with him. Jerry was along and officially they were on duty. The sheet had not been covered that day and Jerry was determined to make a prostitution arrest.

They wandered aimlessly along Surf Avenue watching the giant toys in action and listening to the dull roar of the ocean in the background. They watched the bally of the side shows—done by tired looking young girls with dead eyes. They stopped at Nathan's and ate hot dogs to the smell of frying hamburger and onion. They listened to the high pitch of the barkers before the dirty, postered peep shows.

They stopped at a mitt camp where a young gypsy girl, done up in brightly colored rags, told Sally's fortune. Then, boldly, she asked Sally for a coin to bless. Sally gave the girl a half-dollar. After mumbling incoherently over it and holding it to the candle light the girl dexterously dropped the coin into her brassiere, all the while smiling brazenly into Sally's eyes. It was a polished performance.

Sally stared at the girl dumbfounded, a smile of amusement and disbelief playing across her face.

"Please, may I have it back?" Sally said.

"For my little baby," the girl said. "He needs food and milk."

Outside, when Sally explained what had happened, Jerry was all for arresting the girl.

"No," Sally protested. "Let the poor thing have it."

"But that's grand larceny," Jerry said, quoting, "Any amount taken from the person at night—"

"If you arrest her I'll refuse to press charges," Sally said firmly.

The little gypsy girl grinned triumphantly from the doorway of the mitt camp as they walked slowly away.

The merry-go-round with its brilliantly colored horses moving rhythmically up and down caught Sally's attention. She clapped her hands childishly and insisted on standing and watching as the bronze figures of the Wurlitzer Military Band thumped out a loud, mechanical, disorganized tune on the organ, chimes and snare and bass drums.

At last they stopped before a sad, wornout cabaret with a neon sign of a bluebird blinking on and off. A giant black Mynah bird, seated in a cage behind the bar, gave a wolf whistle and shrilled, "Hi, Baby," to Sally as they entered. Sally threw back her head and laughed delightedly.

They sat at one of the dirty, cracked tables close to the phony cowboys who were playing guitars and warbling off-tune cowboy songs into a microphone. Their discordant voices blared through the dimness of the cabaret. The proprietor, a bald headed, worried little man took their orders.

"How's business?" Jerry said, grinning his tight, knowing grin.

"Terrible," the proprietor moaned. "This dump is costing me a thousand a week and who comes in here? Nobody but those damned girls who buy one coke and sit and make goo- goo eyes at the cowboys all night."

The proprietor, whose name was Sam, shrugged his narrow shoulders with a hopeless look that said, what can you do? He hurried away to fill their order.

"Cheerful guy," Steve said, nudging Sally.

"Look," Sally said, excitedly.

A dwarf had suddenly jumped onto the platform with the cowboys. He brushed them aside with his short, bowed arms and clapped his hands for attention.

A fat young girl who had been singing with the cowboys reached down to gather the dwarf up in her plump arms. The dwarf protested lustily, shouting obscenities in an incongruously deep voice, all the while kicking and punching at her furiously with his small square limbs.

"Let me down, you bitch," he howled. "Stop trying to steal my act."

The fat young girl dropped him to the platform and pouted. She walked huffily off the stage. She sat at the table next to theirs mumbling to herself as the dwarf dragged a chair onto the stage and removed a thick leather belt from his trousers. As the cowboys strummed away at the guitars he beat the chair frantically with his belt all the while staring hard and angrily at the plump girl entertainer. She turned her back to him and spoke to Jerry.

"He's no showman," she said, angrily. "Ain't got no sense of showmanship. I could teach him but he won't let me." She began to cry, large tears rolling down her cheeks, making untidy streaks in the caked powder on her face and smearing the black mascara of her eyes so that she looked grotesque.

Jerry ordered a drink for her which she gulped down without a word. She began to cry again the moment the drink was finished.

Jerry ordered her another drink. "Take it easy," he said, patting her bare fat back consolingly.

"Ten years I been in this business," she blurted out uncontrollably. "Ten years and I never met a guy like him."

The dwarf had now worked himself into a sweat. He stopped beating the chair suddenly, bowed to the applause, replaced his belt and jumped agilely from the stage. He spit in the direction of the fat girl and thumped out of the cabaret on his little bowed legs.

The fat young girl shook her head sadly. "And to think how I love that guy," she confided to Jerry.

"It's really very tragic," Sally said, rocking with suppressed laughter.

"Yeah," Steve said, smiling.

At last the fat girl gathered up her coat and went in search of her lover.

"Steve, don't look now," Jerry whispered, "but I think I got something over there."

Steve sipped his drink for a moment and turned his glance slowly toward the other side of the room. A tall, handsome Negro girl smiled in their direction. Steve saw her wink to Jerry.

"I'm going to give it a try," Jerry said, winking back at the girl. "You wait here till I get back."

Jerry rose and sauntered leisurely from the cabaret. The Negro girl rose quickly and followed him outside. Steve watched as they talked briefly and headed for Jerry's car.

"That's it," Steve said to Sally.

"What?" Sally said. She had been watching the entertainers.

"Jerry just made a contact with a prost," Steve explained.

"How do you know she's a prostitute?" Sally said, looking at him resentfully.

"No pocketbook," Steve said. "The prosts never carry pocketbooks down here."

He watched as the girl got in the car with Jerry.

"Sally," he said, quietly, "all right if you take a cab home? Jerry will be back with her in a few minutes and we'll have to bring her to the precinct for search and booking."

"Of course, Steve," she said, quickly. She shivered slightly.

"You don't mind?"

"Of course not."

She pecked at his cheek quickly.

He called a cab for Sally, gave the cabbie a bill, and smiled as she threw a brief kiss to him from the cab window.

In a moment he was standing alone outside the cabaret waiting for Jerry to return.

A young girl with good legs and a thin dress tried to pick him up but he ignored her. She walked huffily away, but she turned around suddenly and shouted back at him, "You no-good bum!"

He smiled tightly and looked the other way. He was doing her a favor and she didn't know it. He wanted no prostitution pinches for a long time.

Steve was becoming impatient when Jerry drove up in the car alone.

"What happened?" Steve said.

Jerry dabbed at his face with a handkerchief.

"Take a look," he said, turning his face toward Steve. There were three long scratches on the side of his face reaching from his ear to his chin.

"Wow!" Steve gasped. "You picked yourself a wildcat."

"Yeah."

Jerry shifted the car into gear and made an abrupt U-turn. "Gave her five bucks and she wanted me to take her to some furnished room. Soon as she gave me the address I identified myself as a cop. She grabbed me in a half-nelson, clawed my face and jumped out of the car. I chased her and fell and ripped my pants." He pointed to a long tear in his trouser leg.

"Couldn't you catch her?"

Steve was roaring with laughter.

"Sure I caught her," Jerry said, glaring at him. "She ran like a deer but I caught her."

"Where is she now?"

"One of the uniformed boys is holding her for me. I had to come back for you."

They stopped and picked the girl up. She sat silently in the car between them all the way to the precinct station house.

At the station house they booked her for soliciting for purposes of prostitution and for resisting arrest and brought her to the policewoman's room for search.

In a moment the policewoman emerged from the room shouting excitedly for them.

"Hey," she called, excitedly. "Come here quick, you guys."

They raced to the room.

The policewoman pointed to two large, inflated balloons on the desk.

"She's a man," the policewoman exclaimed.

The man stood flatchested in his woman's clothing.

"For Christ's sakes," Jerry said.

They brought the prisoner back to the desk.

"Gotta change the charge, Lieutenant," Jerry said, pushing the prisoner against the desk railing. "This is a fag."

The lieutenant stared seriously at the man in his woman's clothing.

"Policewoman did a search?"

"Hell, no," Jerry said, holding up the balloons. "This is as far as she got."

The lieutenant nodded.

"All right," he said, dryly. "Assault, impersonating a man and soliciting for lewd and indecent purposes. How's that?"

"Good," Jerry said.

"I want a lawyer," the prisoner suddenly shouted.

"You'll get a lawyer," the desk lieutenant said, sharply. He rang for the attendant.

"After he's fingerprinted, put this guy in a cell," he directed.

Outside Steve and Jerry headed for the nearest bar and had a stiff drink together.

This was some hell of a job. Wait till he told Sally about this! She would have another whole chapter for her thesis in Sociology.

CHAPTER SEVEN

THEY drove slowly down a cement ramp to where groups of old warehouses clustered close to a freight yard. Although it was only three o'clock, it was getting dark and heavy black clouds scudded low in the sky. The air already smelled of rain.

They left the car, flashlights in hand, and climbed carefully up a rusty ladder to the top of the tallest warehouse, flattening themselves on the dirty, rusted roof.

"There it is," Steve said, pointing out a huge building directly across from the freight yards. Four men in shirtsleeves sat around a table in a quiet game of cards on the first floor. On the floor above, white venetian blinds were closed tightly against the windows.

"According to information," Steve said, "the policy bank is in the apartment with the venetian blinds."

"Three-thirty," Bob Sherman said, "the policy drops are all going like mad." His voice was harsh and unpleasant, and for some reason Steve didn't like working with him but Jerry was out sick and Bob had been assigned to assist him in running down the policy bank.

Bob Sherman was a slight, morose man of thirty. He was bone thin with a bulging forehead, a receding hairline and a thin blade of a nose. He didn't mix with the men and seldom spent any time around the headquarters of the Vice Squad.

Several times as Steve and Jerry were working on a suspected bookmaker they saw Bob apparently fingering them to the bookie. Time and again they ran into Bob at various bars around the city drinking and talking chummily in the back room with known gamblers and racketeers. Other men in the Vice Squad had had similar experiences with him, and the entire squad was waiting for Bob to make his one big, inevitable mistake.

However, Bob continued to make his share of arrests each month and he seemed to have a special knack for obtaining evidence that held up in court. His record of convictions was the best in the squad.

It was well known among the men that Bob had taken up with a female bookie and she was using him. Her name was Marie Morales, and there was a long file on her in headquarters. She had been officially dubbed a known gambler. She was a tall, plump woman in her late twenties with an ingenuous child's face and the mind of an adding machine. He apparently was giving her information concerning the Vice Squad movements. Prior to Bob's taking up with her she had been pinched at the rate of once a month but since she and Bob had gotten together it had been impossible to get anything on her to justify an arrest.

Bob gripped Steve's arm nervously with a bony hand.

"There's someone in there," Bob hissed, pointing to where a dull stream of light filtered from between the white blinds.

"Uhuh," Steve grunted.

As they watched, a man sidled up to the building, lit a cigarette, glanced furtively up and down the street and then slipped quickly into a basement door of the building.

"Looks good," Bob said, eagerly.

"That was a pigeon, all right," Steve agreed.

Soon a dozen furtive men had entered and left the building in the space of an hour. Their actions were always the same, the lighting of the cigarette, the brief survey of the street and then the hurried entry into the building.

"Those guys act like they're loaded," Bob said.

"They sure do," Steve agreed, glancing at the small, thin man at his side.

It became a kind of sixth sense among plain-clothesmen to recognize the tension of a man carrying horse tickets or policy slips. The most casual of them always made some suspicious move that gave them away.

"Whose bank is it supposed to be?" Bob asked. His eyes were a peculiar yellow brown and seemed always too bright.

Steve shrugged his shoulders non-committally.

"Search me," he said.

He knew all right. It was Lefty Gomez' bank. But he didn't intend confiding his knowledge to Bob. He wanted no tipoff going out to Lefty. That bum had a way of reaching men like Bob. Lately Lefty Gomez had gone underground but he was still financing the policy banks in at least two boroughs.

The Police Commissioner's squad was after Lefty and the D.A. wanted him for questioning. The taking of a Gomez policy bank would be quite a feather in the headquarters squad's cap, and Steve didn't intend to let Sherman louse things up.

All the while they spoke in whispers they kept the house and street under surveillance. The thing was falling into a definite pattern. The men invariably emerged within five to ten minutes after entering the building, just long enough to get rid of the work and the money and have it checked. When the men left they were visibly relaxed and sauntered leisurely up the street away from the building. They seemed to be spacing their approach to the building. Never more than one man approached at any one time and a period of five minutes would pass before the next man approached. Several times the man leaving the building would encounter a man waiting on the corner for his turn. They never spoke or gave any sign of recognition. It seemed evident that these numbers pick-up men, if they were pick-up men, did not even know each other.

"Is there a phone in the building?" Bob asked.

"No. I checked that angle right away."

Suddenly the rain-laden air was pierced with the wild sound of a police siren. The light in the building went out immediately and a shadowy face peered through the slats of the blinds into the street. The men who had been playing cards came to the window and peered out. A runner who had just turned the corner headed for the building, turned abruptly and walked swiftly in the opposite direction.

A sleek black Lincoln, without any lights showing, screeched around the corner on two wheels and headed toward the cement ramp leading to the freight yards. The Lincoln sped down the ramp at top speed, coming to an abrupt halt behind a line of freights.

The police prowl car sped around the corner with its siren going full blast and its red lights blinking frantically on and off and sped down the road past the ramp away from the freight yards. In a moment the police car was back, rolling slowly now. A uniformed man stepped from the car and briefly surveyed the yard from the ramp. He could see nothing from that angle.

Steve and Bob debated on signalling to the uniformed man but decided against it. He might mistake them for hoods and even take a shot at them. After all they were in civilian clothes. And revealing themselves at this time would destroy any chance they might have of taking the policy bank across the street.

The uniformed man returned slowly to the prowl car, shaking his head in a puzzled way. He stepped into the car, slammed the door loudly and the prowl car drove silently away.

The men who had been playing cards left their game. They conferred among themselves and soon the light went out and they emerged in a group from the building, talked briefly on the corner and walked away. There was no light behind the white blinds now. The place had gone completely dead. There was a rear exit from the building, and the men on the floor above had probably taken it, escaping through the tangled alleyways, and were well out of the area by now.

"Well, that's all for them tonight," Bob said.

Steve had already taken his .38 Colt Cobra from its shoulder holster. The cool feel of the metal was reassuring. It was a tiny, efficient weapon.

"Let's get that guy in the Lincoln," he said, crisply.

"Aw, forget him," Bob said. "He's a uniformed force problem."

"He's our problem now," Steve said.

Steve moved quickly to the rusty ladder and, hugging close to its rungs, he let himself down very quietly. Bob cat-footed after him.

"Hope he's not armed," Bob said.

"We'll find out soon enough," Steve said.

As they circled the line of freights the arched neck of the watertower pipe shot upward. The train whistled shrilly. Short, explosive snorts came from the squat funnel of the engine up ahead. The bell began to clank furiously. The train jerked forward, the couplings shrieked and the heavy wheels ground slowly forward.

The train rattled ahead, picking up speed with each jerk.

"Now," Steve shouted above the noise. "I'll take the driver's side."

"Okay," Bob shouted.

Gun in one hand, searchlight in the other Steve dashed to the car.

The swarthy man crouched at the wheel was taken completely unawares.

"Don't shoot," he shouted hoarsely. "I'll get out."

The door swung open and he slipped to the ground.

"Don't move," Steve shouted. "Keep your hands where they are."

The man froze. He was a tall, well-dressed man about fifty.

"Cover me, Bob," Steve said, as he slipped his gun into his pocket.

"He's covered," Bob said, standing close behind Steve.

Without glancing around Steve systematically searched the man. As he touched the man's legs the man grunted, made an abrupt move with his right hand and a shot rang out. The bullet whined over Steve's head and thudded into soft flesh. The man gasped, grabbed for his heart and then he was dead. He stood there momentarily no longer a man but a corpse and he was still standing. Suddenly he crumpled and fell face forward to the cinder and shale strewn ground.

Steve jumped up and played his flashlight over Bob's face. The man looked positively ecstatic.

Steve lurched toward him. Everything was out of focus and turning in tight circles. Suddenly the circles dissolved. He had Bob pinned against the car and was pounding his fist into Bob's surprised face. Blood was dripping from Bob's battered nose.

"You murdering son-of-a-bitch," Steve hissed from between clenched teeth.

Bob's bony knee came up fast but Steve side-stepped and hooked his big fist deep into Bob's wiry body. Bob slumped to the ground gasping for air.

Steve stared down at the crumpled mess at his feet. He shrugged his big shoulders hopelessly. He couldn't explain what he had done. Bob had thought the man was going for a gun. In that split second of decision he had decided to kill the man; Bob was a crack shot and he could have fired above the man's head or at the shoulder but he had sent the bullet right through the heart. Yet the man had moved suddenly. That could have made the difference.

"All right, get up," he said, grabbing Bob by the shoulders and lifting him to his feet.

Bob stood unsteadily, breathing hard and fingering his battered nose.

"You crazy bastard," Bob snarled. "He was going for his gun."

"He had no gun," Steve said, dryly.

He didn't want to talk. "Let's search the car."

Suddenly Bob shouted, "Hey, look at this."

He dragged a large, expensive looking briefcase out from under the front seat.

Steve held his flashlight on it as Bob opened the case.

It contained a thick leather wallet and several small black velvet bags.

Bob emptied the wallet first and whistled softly. He counted the money. More than ten thousand dollars in new, crisp one hundred dollar bills.

"We turn them in," Steve said at once.

Bob's peculiar eyes studied him. They held a question.

"Be reasonable," Bob said at last. "This guy probably stole the money anyway."

"You want to compound the theft?"

"Hell, no," Bob said, aghast. "But look at it this way. You're a bachelor and I got four kids and a wife to support. We don't get much pay and here's a chance to have a little something for ourselves. What say? We split and nobody will be any the wiser."

"No dice," Steve said.

He reached over and took the money and wallet from Bob's hand. The action was so swift Bob had no chance to protest.

"Look in the bags," Steve said, directing his flashlight to the black velvet bags.

They were filled with uncut stones that shone like diamonds.

Bob poured out a handful, holding them longingly in his thin hand. "Stolen, I'll bet," he said, letting them dribble reluctantly back into the bag.

A gun barked and a bullet whined over their heads and ricocheted off the top of the car.

They both fell instantly to the ground beside the auto and the dead man.

"Stay where you are or we'll kill you," a voice shouted out of the darkness.

Suddenly a spotlight coned its way through the muddy darkness and they could see they were surrounded by police prowl cars and uniformed men.

"Hey, we're cops," Bob shouted from his position on the ground. Neither of them moved.

At last two uniformed men and a sergeant approached them cautiously.

"Stand up."

They rose quickly to their feet.

"We're from Headquarters Squad," Steve said, holding his hands in the air. "Shield's in my coat pocket."

The guns didn't move and the searchlights held fast.

"Search him," the sergeant commanded one of the uniformed men.

Heavy hands went through his pockets and found his gun and shield.

"We were on the roof over there," Bob explained, nervously. "We saw this guy ditch the sector car and so we came down to get him. He tried to attack us and we shot him."

"They both have guns and shields, Sarge," the uniformed man who had searched them called.

The sergeant's face relaxed visibly and the uniformed men waited for orders.

"Give them back their shields and guns," he said.

The sergeant turned around and shouted.

"Kelly, take a look at that plate. Check it with your alarms. See if the car is stolen."

A heavy-set patrolman went to the rear of the Lincoln and checked the plate with the alarms written in his memorandum book.

"Stolen, Sarge," he confirmed.

Steve and Bob heaved a sigh of relief. The dead man was no good. The killing was justifiable homicide. Instead of being kicked off the force and brought up on murder charges they now stood in line for departmental recognition.

"You guys go through him?" the sergeant asked.

He was a tall man with a lined, leather-like face and unbelievably cold blue eyes that didn't believe anything.

"Yes," Steve said. "Him and the car."

"Find anything?"

Steve handed over the wallet and the money.

"There's some kind of uncut stones in those bags on the seat," he volunteered.

"Get them, Murphy," the sergeant said to the uniformed man at his side.

"Roach, get back to your car and call Central. Notify the Medical Examiner we got a stiff for him."

The sergeant scanned the ground with his flashlight.

"He have a gun on him?"

"Didn't find any, Sarge," Bob said.

The sergeant turned to the men who were standing around the corpse.

"Spread out, fellows," he said. "Search for a gun. He must have tossed it around here somewhere."

They found the gun between two railroad ties. It was a small, foreign made automatic.

"You guys did a good job," the sergeant said.

"Thanks, Sarge," Bob said.

They waited until the Medical Examiner showed and released the body to the morgue wagon and then they drove to the precinct to be interviewed by the captain who had been called back to work from his home.

Three hours later Steve was alone in his car with the precinct behind him. He and Bob Sherman had told their story of Blinky Randazzo's death while the powerful jawed, gray haired captain listened thoughtfully and then recommended them for departmental recognition. Departmental records indicated Randazzo had a record of assault and robbery dating back almost thirty years and was currently wanted for larceny of the Lincoln and robbery of a Fifth Avenue jewelry shop.

Steve listened to the gasp and click of the windshield wipers as they fought their losing battle against the rain that swept across the car in blinding sheets. They had better not stop. If they did, he felt something inside him would stop. What it was he couldn't tell, but those wipers had better keep going.

He was listening to the dry, low purr of the motor as the car sped along. He pressed harder on the accelerator and the car surged forward. The speedometer needle shot to sixty-five. He released the pedal and the car idled along until the needle dropped to twenty.

He could think of nothing to compare with being alone at night in a car in the rain. This was loneliness complete and absolute. And, somehow, he was glad.

Suddenly a horn blared and a Cadillac swept out of the darkness to cut him off. He swerved to the curb in the glare of a street light. The Cadillac stopped in front of him and a small, bowlegged man with a cap and a trenchcoat jumped from the car and raced through the rain to him.

The man banged on the window. Steve removed his revolver from his armpit and slipped it into his pocket. It was a nice thing to have around. He kept his hand firmly around the butt of the revolver, his index finger touching the trigger lightly.

"Hey," the little man bawled through the window, the rain spattering his face. "You Steve Hochuli?"

Steve looked into the small, rat-like eyes.

"Yes," he said. "Who the hell are you cutting me off like that?"

"Save it," the little man rasped. "The boss wants to see you?"

"What boss?"

But the little man was already racing back to the car.

Steve sat back, fingering the gun in his pocket, and waited.

He watched as a soft-solid figure, clothed in a form fitting blue topcoat and wearing a large pearl gray hat shuffled over to his car.

Soon the man was banging on the window—a dark, mahogany faced man peering through the glass at him.

"Who the hell are you?" Steve said.

"Lefty Gomez." The voice was low and harsh and guttural. "Let me in."

Steve unlocked the door and opened it with his free hand. He shifted the gun in his pocket so that it covered the man, aimed right at his fat heart.

The bow-legged man was back now trying to get in the back door.

"Get the hell out of here," Steve commanded.

"Go ahead," the big man said, nodding his head with the pearl gray hat back toward the Cadillac. The little man raced obediently back to the car as Lefty shifted his bulk into the seat next to Steve.

He held out a fat, pudgy hand.

"Hello, Hochuli," he said, quietly.

Steve ignored the proferred hand.

"What do you want?"

The jowly face took on a pained look. The small black eyes shone like those of an animal.

"I want to talk to you."

"Go ahead, talk."

Steve shifted the gun again so that it pressed into the fat man's side.

Lefty Gomez threw back his big head and laughed. "Don't trust me, eh?" he said, kiddingly.

"No."

"Makes me feel uncomfortable," Lefty said, nodding down toward the gun.

"Too bad. Talk."

Lefty folded his fat hands on his lap and shifted gingerly away from the gun.

"You was down at my bank on Water Street today," he said, slowly. "That right?"

Bob Sherman's image flashed through Steve's mind. The dirty, little stoolie.

"Tell me more."

"The place across from the freight yards."

"Yes, I was there," Steve said. "Who told you?"

"Bob," the big man's eyes flashed. "We're old friends."

"Very cozy," Steve said, studying the big man's heavy, leather face.

"He understands," Lefty said, taking out a toothpick and picking nervously at his yellow teeth with it.

"Understands what?"

Lefty's big shoulders shrugged, and his mean eyes tried to look sorrowful.

"The plight of my people," Lefty went on. "I'm Puerto Rican and my people come here and starve. They can't speak English and they have little education. It is difficult for them to find work and stay off welfare."

"Mr. Bountiful," Steve interrupted. "You give them all jobs, is that it?"

"Yes," Lefty seized on the words. "I give as many as I can jobs. I keep them from starving and from going on welfare. Instead of killing or stealing and maybe getting on the stuff, they work for me. When they are arrested I put up bond, pay the lawyers and the fines."

Out of the goodness of your heart, Steve thought.

"Go on," he said, neutrally.

"I got a little policy business," Lefty continued, deprecatingly. "Not much. Just local stuff."

A reputed five million dollar a year business with spots in every borough of the city and extending as far as New Jersey. Sure, just local stuff.

"I deal square with my people and the players. Nobody gets cheated. They win, I pay off."

They lose, Steve thought, and you collect which is most of the time with the odds a thousand to one against anybody winning. This bird talked as though running the vicious policy racket was legal and he had a license.

"Just a small business," Lefty said, sentimentally. "But I keep my countrymen off welfare. I give them work. If they go to jail I take care of their families. Nobody works for me goes hungry. By doing that I make more money available for raises for you cops."

Steve was lost in the impenetrable jungle of Lefty Gomez's slobbering, sentimental rationalizations. The man seemed to believe all that nonsense himself. Lefty was careful to omit that he controlled a syndicate for prostitutes and that he controlled houses that stretched half way across the country. And those houses were loaded with nice, young Puerto Rican girls who didn't dare open their mouths for fear they would be murdered.

"What do you want?" Steve said, at last.

Lefty offered him a large cigar which he refused. He removed the toothpick from his mouth, broke it and tossed the ends out the window. He stared meditatively at the cigar and then bit off the end, stuffing the cigar into his fat mouth. He took out a gold cigarette lighter and carefully lit the cigar, blowing clouds of smoke leisurely against the moist windshield.

Suddenly he reached into his pocket and pulled out a thick wad of bills. Steve had never seen so much money in his life. The fat brown hands carefully peeled ten one hundred dollar bills from the top of the roll. He tried to press the bills into Steve's hand.

"Put it away, Lefty, I don't take," Steve said, quietly.

It was a big temptation but he wanted nothing to do with this pig of a man. He had a long way to go in the Police Department and he had no intentions of letting a bum like this upset his applecart.

Lefty stared at him with his little pitiless eyes. They were filled with disbelief.

"I take care of everybody," he said, smoothly.

"You're lying in your teeth," Steve countered. "In my book you stink."

Steve's finger itched on the trigger. One slug into that fat hide ... if only the guy would give him some cause. Make a wrong move. But Lefty wasn't making any moves at all in a physical way.

He put the roll back in his pocket and placed his left hand over a place where his heart could have been and raised his right hand dramatically into the air, his small eyes rolling skyward. "By God!" he cried. "They hang me by my heels I don't talk. Nobody breaks Lefty down. Nobody makes Lefty talk. I not like that bum Gross. They kill me I no talk. I level with you, Hochuli. Ask Bob, he tell you."

Steve knew Lefty had been arrested twice for homicide. Twice they got nothing out of him and all the witnesses had either been killed or had discreetly moved away and could not be located.

Steve swore silently. If only he had something on this fat boy that would stand up. He could lock him up for attempted bribery but he would probably be kicked out of the department for even letting the bum talk to him. He could lock him up for vagrancy but he would be out on the streets tomorrow. You had to have evidence, real, concrete evidence—and he had none. Still his curiosity was piqued. Why had Lefty offered him a thousand dollars? Surely it was not merely to show he meant to be friendly.

"What's on your mind?" Steve said, at last.

"Tell me who your stoolie is," Lefty said bluntly. His little eyes were filled with an animal hatred. His voice was low and rasping and pleading. "The one who gave up my bank. Just his name."

Benny the Jockey would sure love to hear this conversation. It would kick him right in the heart. A thousand dollars offered for Benny's life.

"You're wasting your time," Steve said.

Lefty sighed heavily and puffed thoughtfully at his cigar.

"I got friends, Hochuli," he said, ominously. "I break you just like that. You not in plain-clothes no more. Maybe I send you to the Bronx or Staten Island. You rot in those places. Nobody knows or cares about you." He snapped his fat fingers and they gave off a dry, hard sound.

Steve reached across the man's bulk and swung the door open.

"Get out, fat boy," he snapped. "Get out before I kill you."

He locked his fingers in the collar of the big man's coat and heaved him toward the door. Then he brought up a foot against the enormous rump and pushed the great bulk out of the car like a giant football.

Lefty Gomez sprawled grotesquely on the wet cobblestones, his little eyes bugging in disbelief, his pearl gray hat tumbling into the muddy waters along the curb.

He screamed in Spanish and the little bow-legged man came racing from the car through the rain. He helped Lefty to his feet. Lefty stood there shakily.

"I get you, Hochuli," he screamed, waving his fat hand at Steve. "I get you."

"I'll give you two minutes to get out of here," Steve said, quietly. "Then I lock you both up for disconduct."

Steve stepped from his car and held his gun plainly visible in his hand, hammer cocked and index finger touching lightly on the trigger.

He grinned as the big, soft-solid man and the little man hurried to the Cadillac. The motor of the big car roared and the car sped off. He sat and watched the red rear lights disappear.

Suddenly he broke into a cold sweat. Trembling, he quickly replaced the gun in its holster

He started his car and drove aimlessly about for a half hour. Finally he headed the car toward Water Street and the freight yards.

He stopped at the house where Lefty Gomez's policy bank had been. The windows were all boarded up and there was a large FOR SALE sign plastered over the front door. Well, he would have to get Benny the Jockey busy locating that bank again.

He headed for a bar and it wasn't until he'd had half a dozen shots that he felt anything like himself again.

Steve was awakened late the next morning by the telephone. It was his day off and he was going to spend it with Sally.

He answered the phone in a low, sleepy voice. It was Jerry Brickley. Jerry's voice sounded small and nervous over the wire.

"Steve," Jerry was saying. "Get down to the office right away—it's important."

"What's the big secret?"

"Can't talk. Get down here."

The receiver clicked.

Steve had a brief feeling of panic. Something was wrong. It took a great deal to excite Jerry and he was definitely upset about something.

He called Sally and cancelled their date. She was disappointed and made no effort to hide her feelings. Well, he would make it up to her some other time.

When he arrived at Headquarters, Charlie Quinlan, the mild mannered lieutenant, ushered him quickly into the Chief's office. The entire plain-clothes staff was standing at attention in front of the Chief. The place was airless and silent and tense.

The lieutenant took a chair on the right side of the desk, and the men waited expectantly.

Assistant Chief Inspector Mike Rossetti glowered at the men from beneath his glasses. The flat, depthless eyes looked at all of them but saw no one. His open, ruddy face was flushed a deep red. He raised a thick hand to his head and flattened down the two locks of dyed hair that covered the top of his shiny scalp.

"Men," he boomed out suddenly. "I'm sorry I had to call you here this morning. I know some of you worked last night and I know others are on their day off. However," he shrugged his heavy shoulders, "I got a situation here I want to straighten out once and for all."

A restless stir went through the assembled men.

"What's he leading up to?" Steve whispered to Jerry, who was standing against the wall in the back.

"Beats me," Jerry said.

"Me, I'm the general," the Chief was saying, lighting a cigar and waving it out at them. "You're my men because I hand picked each of you. I took you out of uniform and gave each of you the best job this department could offer. That right?"

"Right, Chief," they answered in unison.

"Now, men," the Chief continued, ponderously. "I know most of you are out there in the field doing your best and I appreciate it. Now, how do I know you are good men? First, you keep the sheet covered. Not one of you has fallen down on your arrests—and they are damned good ones, believe me. Secondly, there has never even been one hint of graft or corruption in the Headquarters Squad. No letters, no civilian complaints. You are all good men—competent men and I'm pleased to work with you."

The Chief waved his short, heavy arm at them and his cigar fell unceremoniously to the floor. The Chief glared at the men, daring them to so much as snicker.

"Now, listen close, I want everybody to hear this," the Chief continued with deceptive frankness. "How many of you men have heard of Lefty Gomez?"

There was a chorus of, "We know him, Chief."

The Chief nodded his big head. "Good," he said. "I'm glad you're up on your known gamblers. Now," he paused dramatically. "I'm not trying to trap any of you but I want straight answers. Have any of you men ever taken any money from him?"

The men remained silent and rigid.

The Chief's open, ruddy face broke into a good-natured grin, but nobody was fooled. He was boiling. He hadn't called them all in merely to compliment them on their good work and honesty.

Suddenly the Chief turned to Bob Sherman, who stood huddled in a corner near the window.

"How about you, Bob," he said, casually. "You ever take any money from Lefty Gomez?"

Bob's bony face broke out into sweat and his thin blade of a nose quivered uncontrollably. A muscle somewhere behind his jaw twitched.

"No, sir," he whispered in a hardly audible voice.

The Chief fumbled with a sheaf of papers on his desk.

"Know what this is, Bob?" he said, holding the white, type-written papers high in his spatulated fingers.

"No, sir," Bob said in a dry, tangled voice.

"This," the Chief said, letting the papers flop to his desk, "is a copy of Lefty Gomez' statement to the District Attorney."

The Chief addressed the assembled men again. "You guys don't know it yet—or maybe some of you do," he amended, "but the District Attorney's office took Lefty Gomez' operation this morning and they grabbed Lefty and he's talking his head off. And for your information, Bob," he continued, grimly, "he named you as one of the men he paid off."

Bob paled and sighed audibly, shifting uncomfortably from one foot to the other.

"It's a lie," he whispered. "I never took a dime from him."

"It's a lie," the Chief boomed angrily. "I wish it was a lie. But it ain't. The District Attorney had your picture too and a couple of good recordings of your voice taken from a tap on Lefty Gomez' home telephone. Bet you didn't know you were a recording and television star, did you, Bob?"

Bob rubbed a pale hand across his bulging forehead where the hard blue veins were plainly visible now pushing up from the skin. He said nothing.

"By tonight you'll be known from coast-to-coast," the Chief continued dryly, "as the one cop in my Squad who is a grafting, corrupt liar."

Bob looked as though he was about to faint.

"One of you fellows get him a chair," the Chief commanded.

A chair was brought in and Bob was seated facing the Chief. He seemed terribly huddled and small in the chair.

"I suppose you think I'll try to help you," the Chief said, glaring at Bob.

"No, sir," Bob mumbled.

"No, sir, is right," the Chief shouted. "I told the D.A. you were his baby and if he wanted to turn you over to the Grand Jury for investigation that was all right with me."

"Can I go now, Chief?" Bob said, trying to rise from the chair.

"No, damn you, you can't go. Just sit right where you are.

"Twenty-eight years to build a reputation in this department and one cop like you can ruin it," the Chief fumed. "I'm not going to let you do it, Sherman, not by a long shot."

Steve remembered back to his first interview with the Chief. The Chief had referred to himself as 'The Whip,' 'The Big Whip.' Well, he hadn't exaggerated. He was whipping Bob Sherman to a pulp. Steve had no sympathy for Bob or what he had done but he felt the Chief was overdoing the whole thing, exaggerating it all out of proportion. He knew he was using Bob as a whipping boy to keep the men in line—but this was enough. They all got the idea.

"I'm going to send you to jail, Sherman," the Chief shouted, pointing his short, heavy finger at Bob.

Bob shrank further into the chair.

"And you know why? Because you didn't just let me down, you gave the whole damned department a black eye. You gave the newspapers another headline to crucify us and you gave another D.A. a chance to be a judge. And why? Why? Weren't you making enough money?"

"I got a wife and four kids," Bob said, showing his first sign of courage.

"What?" the Chief bellowed.

Bob repeated his words.

"So, you're going to hide behind your family. Like hell you are. Nobody made you become a cop. You knew the salary. You knew the conditions. All right. Get up."

Bob rose shakily from the chair.

"Turn around and face these men."

Bob turned, his face deathly pale and his eyes fixed on the floor.

"Now walk. Walk to the clerical officer's desk and pick up the D.A.'s subpoena and get the hell out of this building as fast as you can go."

Never had Steve seen a man so humiliated, so completely chopped to pieces. Somehow, he felt smaller and less human for having witnessed the whole thing.

"That," the Chief said, quietly to the men, "is how any man standing here will be treated if I ever catch him taking a dime from any of these tinhorn bums. Now get out and do your job."

The men, glad to be dismissed, hurried silently from the room.

Two days later the Chief's words became a reality. Bob was indicted by the Grand Jury along with four other officers from the Divisions in which Lefty Gomez bad policy operations.

That evening Bob's picture appeared in the daily papers as one of the corrupt cops who had protected what the D. A. estimated to be a five million dollar a year policy racket.

Later, he and his family became television stars with Bob's picture superimposed beside that of his wife and four children as his wife was interviewed by one of those pitiless news commentators who love to record human misery.

She was a plain, frightened, tiny woman who protested Bob's innocence and said he was "... a good husband, and father and a good provider and that she believed he was innocent."

Later, the same commentator showed films taken by the D.A.'s office of Bob entering several of Lefty Gomez' spots and leaving arm in arm with Lefty. The same man ran off several wiretap recordings of Bob and other cops agreeing to payoffs from Lefty Gomez. No question. Bob and the others were neatly wrapped up and packaged for a three-to-five year trip up the river.

But no mention was made in either the screaming headlines nor in the smaller print beneath of the more than six hundred Vice Squad cops who were not involved in protecting Lefty Gomez's racket kingdom.

Nor were there any comments good, bad or indifferent concerning the more than twenty-thousand police officers who never were nor ever would be involved in corruption or graft.

CHAPTER EIGHT

I T WAS one of those dull nights that come in the middle of the week and they were on the graveyard shift.

The windows of the car were open and the rank summer smells drifted in from the narrow, dirty streets. It was a depressed area of a precinct they seldom worked in. Mostly residential. Not much doing here. Occasional card game, crap game, a little policy but nothing big. Main reason was most of the people didn't even have change to gamble with.

"Hey," Jerry said, suddenly coming to life. "Stop here, Steve. Right behind that black Buick. Don't get too close to the light."

They parked away from the street light. It was a Negro area and the light reflecting off their white skins would be a dead giveaway to anybody looking.

They settled down into the seats with only the tops of their heads visible.

"That house, right side corner," Jerry said.

"Yeah."

"Took a dice game out of there a year ago. Let's sit and watch it for awhile."

"How many did you get?" Steve said.

"Forty—fifty, something like that. Supposed to be peddling moonshine there too but we couldn't locate the stuff."

As they watched two carloads of men stopped in front of the house and laughing and shouting they shuffled up the front steps.

"Looks good, Jerry."

Jerry nodded without speaking.

"I'll go first," Jerry said, after a time, cautiously opening the car door. "First floor right. There's a peephole in the door. When you see me go up the steps, you come after me and stay close to the buildings."

As Jerry went up the steps to the house Steve slipped from the car, closing the door noiselessly. He hugged the buildings, his shadow mingling with those of the tall tenement houses and brownstones. Soon he was in the hallway.

Jerry was crouched down by the door with the peephole. Steve stepped cautiously along the wornout carpeting. Crouching down beside Jerry he listened.

Through the door they could hear the sound of dice being tossed against the wall and the metallic sound of coins being tossed to the floor.

"It's going," Steve said.

"Yeah," Jerry whispered excitedly.

"How are we going to get in there?"

Jerry shook with silent laughter and put a long, slender finger to his lips.

Suddenly he let out a low, agonized moan, following it up by heavy, strangling breathing.

They waited. The game still went on inside. They hadn't heard him. Steve shrugged his shoulders and grinned at Jerry.

"Try again," he whispered.

Jerry took a deep breath and let out the loudest, most agonized groan Steve had ever heard in his life. The game inside stopped instantly. At last Jerry had his audience and he played the part to the hilt. He went wholeheartedly at it, moaning loud, low and long, following it up with strangled breathing. There were muffled, deep voiced conversations inside now. Deep, suspicious voices filled with concern and fear and curiosity. Jerry kept at it, sounding for all the world like someone in the throes of a heart attack.

At last the people inside could stand it no longer. Their curiosity got the better of them. They peered through the peephole but since both Jerry and Steve were crouched low beside the door they could see nothing. The door opened very slowly.

Like two great cats Jerry and Steve leaped into the room among the frightened Negroes.

There on the floor were two great red dice and piles of bills and change.

"Police," Jerry announced, unnecessarily flashing his shield.

"We knows you de law," a tall, good natured Negro said, laughing and showing off a mouthful of magnificent white teeth. "Man, you scared us. We thought you was dying out there the way you sounded."

Everybody laughed.

They continued to laugh and joke as Steve and Jerry methodically collected the evidence. The laughter continued as they searched the drab little kitchen and found a coffee pot filled with moonshine hidden behind the stove. They were still joking and laughing when the patrol wagons came to take them away.

At the precinct the youthful, blond haired desk lieutenant groaned as he saw the prisoners marching in at four o'clock in the morning.

"Don't you guys ever sleep?" he shouted at the prisoners.

"Man, we just couldn't sleep with all the hollering and moaning that was going on outside our door tonight," a prisoner shouted back.

The station house echoed to their laughter as they were lined up against the muster room wall and methodically searched.

"Take them into the sitting room," the lieutenant directed. "Make out the arrest cards."

Steve and Jerry marched the prisoners into the sitting room.

As the prisoners were being seated around the long table in the backroom Steve noticed a young girl stretched out on a bench against the wall, a gray police blanket tucked around her, her head covered by an enormous white bandage that was stained with blood. He walked over slowly and took a good look.

Rusty!

She looked thinner and paler than when he had last seen her. Her eyes were blank and enormous with purple circles under them. One side of her face was covered with dried blood and the bones threatened to push through the thinness of her face.

Her red hair was matted with blood where it fell in untidy streamers from the bandage down the sides of her face. The room seemed filled with her hurt and fear. Even the Negroes had stopped laughing at the sight of her.

"Man, she been gun whipped," one Negro said.

The pupils of her eyes were dilated. There was unbelievable hurt there. I made that face, Steve thought.

The room was hushed and silent now.

"Hello, Rusty," he said slowly.

She whispered something. He leaned close to hear her.

"I hurt," she murmured, pitifully. "I hurt ... Her voice trailed off.

"Who did it, Rusty?" he said.

She seemed not to hear him. Then the eyes came suddenly to life, focussed on him briefly with fear and hostility and then she turned her face to the wall.

"She doesn't like you much," Jerry said.

"Go to hell," Steve said, not looking at him.

He knelt down close to her. "Rusty, listen, I want to help you. Tell me who did it."

She turned her head and stared at him.

"Who did it?" he repeated softly. "Tell me, Rusty."

"I don't know," she whispered, turning away from him.

A squat, imperious-looking woman wearing a white uniform under a blue overcoat and carrying a doctor's black leather bag entered the sitting room.

"Step back, please," she said. Her voice was thick and guttural.

The doctor removed the blanket from a shabby black dress stained with blood. Her silk stockings were all runs and holes and the heel had come off her right shoe. There was a livid bruise on her right knee.

The doctor spoke softly, reassuringly to Rusty as she cleaned the wounds and carefully re-bandaged her head.

"The stretcher," the doctor said, matter of factly to the ambulance driver who was standing by.

Steve helped carry her out on the stretcher to the waiting ambulance. He felt as guilty as though he had gun-whipped her himself.

"I'll be around to see you," he promised, in the ambulance.

Her eyes were feverish now. She seemed neither to see nor hear him.

"How bad is she, doctor?" he said, as they stepped from the ambulance.

"Concussion," the doctor said, simply. "Possible fracture. I'll know better after we X-ray. She's in a state of shock now."

He thanked the doctor and returned to the station house to help Jerry with the arrest cards. As he stood in the doorway the ambulance drove off, its siren shrieking into the still night.

Steve sniffed the tinctured, antiseptic air of the hospital ward as he stepped between the rows of white beds on wheels.

The eyes of the patients, crowded into the one tremendous room, followed him.

"Over there," the starched nurse said, pointing to where Rusty was lying, her bandaged head propped up on a white pillow and her child-like figure half-covered by a gray hospital blanket.

She was staring fixedly at the celling. He pulled up a chair and sat beside the bed without a word. For a long time he sat there quietly studying her. Her face had regained some of its youthful coloring but it was still bony and exhausted looking. It was a young-old face where once it had been animated with a youthful exuberance. The tremendous blue eyes contained only a dull wariness.

"Hello, Rusty," he said finally.

"Get me some water," she whispered. Her lips parted only slightly when she spoke.

Steve rose and went to the nurse's desk.

"How is she?" he asked the nurse.

"It's against regulations for you to have the diagnosis."

He stared at her incredulously.

"Can't you tell me anything?" he said.

"Are you related to her?"

"No," he said. Then he added quickly, "I'm her fiance."

"Oh, I see." The dull face broke into a friendly smile. "She's had a severe concussion and fourteen sutures were required to close the wounds on her head." She paused. "However," the ugly mouth continued. "Her condition is good. There was no fracture. She could be released within ten days."

Steve grinned his thanks.

"Is she in any pain?" he said.

"None."

"Can I get her some water," he asked, hesitantly. "She said she wanted water."

"That little room in the corner," the nurse said, pointing across the room. "You'll find a bottle there with her name on it."

Rusty sipped the ice-water through a glass straw. He felt a great sense of relief. At last he was doing something helpful, and she was accepting his help.

He opened the box of candy he had brought. She accepted the chocolate with a small smile and sucked on it for a long time without saying anything.

"What day is it?" she asked suddenly.

"Thursday."

"How long have I been here?"

"A week."

The spark faded from her eyes, and her pale lips moved uneasily. "Did she say when I would get out?"

So she had been watching him and knew he had spoken to the nurse.

"Yes. In ten days."

Her pale lips tried to smile.

Steve shifted uneasily in his chair.

"Would you come with me?" he said, soberly.

She studied him critically.

"Why?" she said. "Why me?"

"Look," he said, excitedly. "I've got a whole apartment to myself. I can take care of you until you're well. Will you come?"

She waited a long time before she spoke, her eyes again on the ceiling.

"Sure," she said, listlessly. "Sure, why not?"

Once outside he felt ridiculously excited and stepped into a bar for a drink.

In between drinks he phoned Sally. Could he come up right away? She hesitated but at last agreed.

He walked quickly up the wide, rug-covered steps to her apartment, feeling guilty for what he was about to do. For weeks now he had been coming here, two, three, four times a week. He knocked on the door.

"Come!" Sally's twangy voice sounded through the door.

He entered to find Sally sitting at her desk on the opposite side of the living room, a typewriter before her and a pile of manuscript paper and a book to one side of the machine.

"Hi, lover," she said, glancing up with a grin.

She stared at him. Instantly she knew something had changed with him.

"Steve!" she said.

She rose quickly, taking off the reading glasses she always wore when typing.

"Steve, what's the matter with you?"

"Nothing," he said, grinning sheepishly. "Just had a few drinks."

She took his coat and he settled down familiarly on the old sofa.

He studied her grave eyes, the good cheekbones and the full mouth he had kissed so often.

"I'm interrupting your studies," he said, half-apologetically.

"Nonsense," she said, making a deprecating gesture. "They can wait."

He hesitated. He had never told Sally anything about Rusty. She didn't even know Rusty existed. He didn't like scenes. He hoped Sally would understand how it was.

And then he plunged into the story of Rusty. She listened quietly as he spoke, her eyes lighting up with interest as he told of the arrest. He gave her a detailed description of Rusty, her background, the man, Tony, she had gone away with and Rusty's present condition.

When he finished Sally smiled a little stiffly at him.

"Don't worry," she said, gently. "I'll live. Thanks for telling me about it."

When he left, she patted his arm affectionately, but pushed him firmly away when he bent to kiss her.

It had gone off better than he expected, he thought, better than he'd had any right to hope for.

He stopped at several bars, by way of celebration and out of a sense of relief, before he reached home.

The day threatened rain and none of the plainclothesmen wanted to go out on the fishing trip but the Chief insisted. He had chartered the boat and he was damned if a little rain was going to stop him from fishing. The rain had come and they hadn't caught any fish. Now the party boat was struggling mightily through the choppy, wind-tossed waters of the Great South Bay to her dock.

They were clustered around the long table in the cabin listening to the Chief's voice booming above the noise of the waves. The cabin smelled foul of food, cigar smoke and fuel oil.

As the boat, heading for the dock, was caught in the heavy motions of the sea, food, liquor and cigars tumbled to the wet deck. Salt water dribbled down the ladder and sloshed around the deck of the cabin, paper plates and cups and napkins floating around in it. The men braced themselves against the bulkhead and tried to listen.

"I'm the best damned boss you ever had," the Chief was saying. "Ain't that right?"

"Right, Chief," they shouted in unison.

Steve nudged Jerry. "Soon as she hits the dock, I've got to beat it," he whispered.

"Heavy date?" Jerry said.

"Yeah," Steve said.

Steve had deliberately taken a seat at the far end of the table from the Chief and close to the ladder. As soon as the boat docked he intended slipping off and heading straight for the hospital for Rusty. He had been looking forward to it for a week.

"God damn it," the Chief shouted. "Somebody get me a cigar."

The lieutenant seated next to the Chief handed him a fresh cigar.

The Chief fumbled for a newspaper clipping in his jacket pocket.

"I want everybody to hear this," he said. He held the paper unsteadily in front of him and began to read in a deep, blurred voice:

"'At a City Hall ceremony the Mayor presented checks for five hundred dollars to each of ten widows and other survivors of policemen who died on duty this year. The recipients were the first of such survivors to share in the $57,000 raised at the "Salute to the Finest" benefit show at Madison Square Garden on March 17th.'"

There were murmurs around the table.

"Everybody shut up," the Chief shouted, glowering at them.

The cabin was immediately silent. The storm outside seemed to be abating. The rough motion of the sea had stopped and the boat moved easily against the dock.

The Chief puffed his cigar thoughtfully and stared at the men.

"Men," he announced, quietly. "I had a reason for reading this thing to you." He waved the clipping at them and then dramatically crushed it and let it fall to the wet deck. He paused and glanced myopically at the men. His voice went solemn and deep and a little maudlin when he spoke again.

"Bob Sherman committed suicide this morning."

There was a shocked silence. They knew Bob was out on bail and living away from his family.

The Chief nodded his big head solemnly. "Put a gun in his mouth and blew the top of his head off."

The Chief waved his short, heavy arms for silence.

"You know as well as I do," he said, heavily, "a commanding officer is no good unless he commands. Maybe I was pretty hard on Bob, but he had it coming and I don't regret one word I said to him."

The Chief stared at them moodily.

"The reason I read you that thing from *The Times*," the Chief continued, "is that I want each of you to know we don't want handouts and Bob ain't entitled to any. I'm giving his wife and kids five hundred dollars from my own pocket."

Lieutenant Quinlan rose. "I'm adding a hundred to the chief's money," he said.

"How about getting up a fund," one of the plainclothesmen said suddenly. "Say, fifty dollars from each man."

"Good idea," the Chief barked. "Damned good idea." He turned to the lieutenant. "Charlie, you handle this."

The Chief settled back against the bulkhead and went into a whispered conversation with the lieutenant."

"I'm leaving," Steve whispered.

"Go ahead, he's not looking," Jerry said.

Steve slid quickly away from the table and ran up the ladder. He didn't give a damn what measures the Chief felt necessary to soothe his conscience. Rusty was coming home with him to live ....

Rusty was waiting in the hospital waiting room. She was wearing the yellow cashmere sweater and brown skirt he had bought her. Her thick red hair had been cut close so that it formed a ragged cap around her head. Her eyes were even bigger and bluer than he remembered them. The skirt fitted her like a tube from which emerged her slender perfect legs.

Helping her into the car in front of the hospital he touched her hand. It felt smooth and cool and he suddenly became unnerved by his reaction. Merely touching her brought forth a surge of almost uncontrollable desire. All his good plans seemed merely the outgrowth of lust.

As he drove toward home with Rusty sitting next to him erect and silent, her pale face revealing nothing, the words of an old poem, remembered out of childhood, came tumbling into his consciousness.

> *Some say the world will end in fire,*
> *Some say in ice.*
> *From what I've tasted of desire*
> *I hold with those who favor fire.*

He had planned to talk easily with her, but he felt overcome with uncertainty. He remained silent.

And then suddenly they were home. The old, brown shingled house with its boarded up windows stood before them, dark, mysterious and unaccountably hostile.

"This is it," he said, with forced cheerfulness.

She made no reply, but followed him stiffly from the car and into the dark place he called home.

"So this is where you live," she said, at last.

He slipped his arm about her waist, possessively.

"What's the matter with you?" she snapped, moving quickly away from him.

He felt embarrassed and said nothing.

Looking at everything, she walked about the room, teetering on the high heels of the brown shoes he had bought her. Then she glanced distrustfully up at the stern portrait of his grandfather, hanging above the imitation fireplace.

"Who's that?" she said.

"My grandfather."

"He frightens me."

"Me too," he said, forcing a laugh. "Sit down," he said, quickly. "You look tired."

She settled into a chair with a prolonged sigh, lit a cigarette and stared defiantly for a long time at the portrait.

"Does it bother you so much?" he said, quietly.

"Yes."

She let the cigarette smoke filter slowly from her mouth.

"I'll fix that," he said.

He climbed up on a chair and took the portrait down and concealed it behind a chair.

"That better?" he said, smiling at her.

The act had pleased him immeasurably. He wondered why he had not thought of doing it before.

"Yes," she said, smiling for the first time.

"Come on," he said, with all the cheerfulness he could summon. "I'll show you around the dump."

He showed her the shabby, little apartment with its moldering furniture of another century and its ancient, barroom smells.

On the bed in his grandparents' room he had placed the blue nightgown and slippers he had bought. She giggled when she saw her things. She even liked the austere brass bed and the gilt framed picture of the bleeding heart that hung so ominously above the head of it.

"I used to be very religious when I was a kid," she confided.

He was secretly amused that Rusty was to sleep in that puritanical bed his grandparents had shared together for more than half a century. He could almost feel their disapproval.

"Don't you ever get lonely here?" she said.

"Sometimes."

"Do you bring many girls here?"

She stared at him with vacuous blue eyes.

"Never," he said.

"I'm the first?"

"Yes."

"I don't believe you."

"Why should I lie to you?" He shrugged to conceal his anger.

And then in a voice tangled with emotion, she relented and tried to thank him but he would not let her. He explained that she could keep the place clean and cook his meals in exchange for her room and board until she got a job. She could leave anytime she felt well enough. He tried to be objective and to present the situation in a businesslike way but it fell flat He fooled neither Rusty nor himself.

Suddenly Rusty laughed, bringing color to her pale face.

"What's so amusing?" he said, lighting his pipe and gazing at her thoughtfully.

"It just struck me funny, that's all," she said.

"What?"

"Me living with the cop that locked me up. Isn't that funny?"

Steve shrugged and made no reply.

They made coffee and in the more friendly atmosphere of the kitchen they were able to talk more freely than they ever had before. The wall between them broke down at last and they were both glad.

"Won't people around here wonder about me?" Rusty asked.

"There's no one but us in the house," he said, quickly. "The places around here are being torn down to make way for the thruway and they're mostly empty. There is no one who will ask any questions."

She sipped her coffee thoughtfully.

"You work a lot nights, don't you?"

"Yes."

"Well, I'm going to be pretty scared around this dump at night all by myself."

He laughed reassuringly.

"There's the phone," he said, pointing to an extension receiver fixed to the kitchen wall. "I'll leave my number. You can call me if anything bothers you."

"But, what'll I do all alone here by myself?"

"Well, there's the television," he suggested, hesitantly.

Rusty laughed childishly.

"You know, I feel just the way I used to when I was a kid and they sent me to a new foster home. Sort of scared and strange."

"You'll get over it," he said, gently. "And as soon as you feel up to it you can look for a job and stand on your own feet."

"Yeah, look for a job," she said, mockingly. "But I haven't any clothes."

"Tomorrow you can go shopping," he said. "I'll give you the money. Buy whatever you need."

She stared at him, frankly puzzled.

"Why?" she said. "Why are you doing this for me?"

"I want to," he said. "I can't explain it. I just want to. Makes me feel good. That's all."

Rusty's head jerked suddenly to one side. She seemed unaware of the movement.

"Are you feeling all right?" he said, anxiously.

"Sure, I'm fine," she said, staring at him in a puzzled way. And then it came to her. "Oh, you mean this," she said, quickly repeating the movement.

"Yes."

"Doctor said a nerve in my neck was injured by the beating I took. Said it would go away after awhile."

"Rusty," he said, hesitantly. "Tell me what happened? Who beat you up like that?"

She gazed at him for a long time without speaking. She seemed to be turning the thing over in her mind and then she shrugged her shoulders in a hopeless way.

"Was it Tony?" he prompted.

She stared at him quizzically. "Yes," she said, finally.

"Why?"

"It's a long story."

"Tell me anyway," he persisted.

Her gaze became suddenly hostile. "I know what you're up to," she said, rising angrily from the chair.

"Sit down," he said, flatly.

She hesitated and then sat down. Lighting a cigarette she blew streams of smoke through her nostrils.

"You're trying to make a stoolie out of me," she said. "That's why you brought me here."

"You know better than that."

She closed her eyes and pressed them lightly with her fingertips.

"Do your eyes bother you?"

"No."

"Want some more coffee?" he said.

"Yes, please."

He poured two more cups of coffee.

"Is there any Scotch in the house?" she said.

He poured her a glass of Scotch and water.

She drank it down greedily.

"Good," she said, her eyes sparkling. "I needed that."

He nodded and remained silent. The question hung between them like a shadow.

"If I tell you what happened, what will you do?"

"I don't know," he said frankly.

He waited patiently.

Rusty fought a losing battle with herself. She knew eventually she would tell him. She had to tell someone. It was better to tell him and get it over with.

"Get me another drink, will you?"

He poured drinks for two and waited.

She gulped down the second drink and lighted a fresh cigarette.

"You know what business Tony was in?"

"No."

"He was a transporter—a white slaver."

"What did you know about Tony before you went with him?" he said, breaking the silence.

"Nothing, only he seemed like a nice guy with lots of money to spend," she said, gazing at the floor.

"What was his full name?"

"Tony Suraci," she said, slowly. "At least that's the name he used."

"When you were with him where did you live?"

She gave him an address in uptown Manhattan.

"Did you live as man and wife. I mean, is that what you told the renting agent?"

"Yes."

"Then you were known as Mrs. Suraci?"

"Yes." She smiled grimly.

He felt a pang of jealousy which he quickly stifled.

"Go ahead," he said, shortly. "What happened?"

"We used to go out cabareting a lot, maybe four times a week. You know, eating out and dancing."

"Did you meet any of his friends?"

"No," she said, quietly. "Never."

"Who paid for all this cabareting?" he said, trying hard to control his mounting anger.

"Tony. He paid for everything—the apartment, my clothes, food and the nights out."

"Just like being married?" Steve said.

"That's right."

He was grimly aware of the parallel and he didn't like it.

"Seems like everybody wants to take care of you."

She laughed shortly. It was a harsh, humorless laugh.

"He wanted to take care of me, all right." She nodded her head in a cynical way and stared up at the ceiling.

"When did you find out Tony was transporting girls to whorehouses?" he asked, bluntly.

"I'm coming to that."

She lit another cigarette, inhaled deeply and sighed.

"One night he came into the apartment and told me I was going to work. At first I didn't get it, so he explained. Tony was very good at explaining. He was taking me to Chicago and putting me into a whorehouse—he thought. I refused to go with him. He gun whipped me until I couldn't stand up. When I was on the floor he kicked me. I just lay there unable to even cry I was so stunned."

"Nice boy," Steve said.

"It wasn't entirely his fault. He belonged to a syndicate and he had to get his quota of girls or else he was out. He told me he liked me—liked me a lot but he didn't have any choice. He had to put me to work. If he didn't, he would not only be out but he might be dead pretty quick. Anyway it came down to him or me and I had to go to work."

"What syndicate?" Steve said. "Did he ever mention any of the guys he worked for?"

"No. He never told me anything about them."

"All right. Go on," Steve prompted.

"Well, after he beat me up I was bleeding pretty badly and aching all over. I managed to crawl into my room and lock the door. He didn't try to stop me. After a while he knocked but I didn't budge. He said he was going out and when he came back I had better be dressed and ready to go with him. He was clearing out that night for Chicago."

"Did he have any spots here in the city?" Steve said. "I mean whorehouses where he supplied the girls?"

"No," she said. "Not that I know of."

"What did you do after he went out?" he said.

"I ducked out and headed straight for the police station. I was pretty badly beaten up and bleeding. I know I looked a mess and I guess I wasn't very coherent when I got there."

"No," Steve said, grimly remembering the broken beaten kid he had seen at the precinct. "You were in pretty sad shape."

Rusty shrugged her shoulders. "That's the whole story." She glanced up at him shamefacedly. "Not very pretty."

"No," he agreed, dryly. "Not very pretty."

Suddenly she placed her head on the kitchen table and what he expected to happen happened. She cried hysterically, her whole body wracked by dry, hot sobs.

"It's all right, Rusty," he said, his hand on hers. "It's all over now."

"I'm such a damned fool," she kept repeating. "Nothing but a damned fool."

"Stop crying."

"I can't," she said, not looking up from the table.

"Oh, for Christ's sake."

He lifted her unprotesting and clinging to him and carried her to the bed. She lay there secret and remote under the bleeding heart with its gilt frame.

"Steve," she whispered. "I lied to you."

"What about?"

"Tony did have a whorehouse he supplied in the city."

"Where?"

"I don't know but he used to call some madam he called Mildred."

"Do you remember the number."

She gave him the number which he hastily scribbled down.

"What are you going to do?" she said, looking at him, her eyes swollen with tears.

"I'm going to work on it," he said. "Maybe we'll dig up Tony."

"He's not a bad guy," she said.

"No," he repeated quietly. "He's not a bad guy."

"Get washed up and go to bed," he said. "I'll see you in the morning."

He left her there sobbing on the old puritanical bed.

He showered and went to bed but he couldn't sleep. He lay on the bed with his eyes closed listening to the traffic going by outside. With what she had told him there was a good chance of picking up Tony Suraci. He would check the departmental records. They might have something on him. If that was his right name. In any case he could trace down the number she had given him and if this Mildred was really a madam they would pick up that end of the operation.

He heard the sound of footsteps in the hall. He held his breath. In a moment she was silhouetted in the doorway.

"Steve," she whispered. "Are you asleep?"

"No."

He turned on his side and watched her.

"I'm scared."

She leaned over the bed and pale light coming through the window picked up the outline of her full, plump breasts pressed against her flimsy nightgown.

"Can I sleep with you?" she whispered.

He reached up and drew her into the bed with him.

Steve spent more than three weeks in an exhaustive search of police records. The search proved fruitless. There was no Tony Suraci listed. The feelers he sent out to the Chicago police and the F.B. I. came back marked, "No Record."

The furnished apartment where Tony had lived with Rusty was now occupied by another couple. The landlady had looked at Steve quizzically and would give him no information. She knew nothing of Tony Suraci, where he had come from nor where he and the girl had gone. The wrinkled monkey face was wily and knowing. Cops were a necessary annoyance in her business.

They revisited the cheap cabarets where Rusty had been with Tony. Steve spoke to the owners, the bartenders and the porters; the men in the combos. He listened to the raucous voices of men and women with vulpine faces and feverish dark eyes, but there was nothing except occasional phrases of meaningless obscenity and filth as they studied the shield he showed them.

He traced the telephone number Rusty had given him to a Mildred Goldberg, who had a place over on West End Avenue. After work he went there. As he walked briskly along West End Avenue he could hear the shrill whistle of a tugboat and the deep horn of an ocean liner in the North River. They lent a note of mystery to the summer night.

A deep blue canopy, stretching from building to curb, identified the building he was looking for. He waited until the doorman stepped to the curb, shrilly blowing on his whistle for a cab for the elderly, respectable looking couple who had emerged from the building. As the doorman spoke to the cabbie, Steve slipped unseen into the building. No point in letting the doorman see him. If Mildred Goldberg was running a whorehouse in the building, she most certainly would have the doorman, the elevator operators and all the other building employees on a monthly pad.

The night clerk behind the reception desk had his back turned to Steve.

He slipped past the closed elevator doors to the mock marble stairs. On the second floor the marble gave way to black steel steps. He went swiftly and silently up the stairs to the fourth floor. On the fourth floor he went searching down the long, heavily carpeted corridor. He found the door leading to Apartment 4G. There, above the pearl button, was the name, Mildred Goldberg. He listened but could bear no sound of movement through the thick door.

He found a broom closet directly across the hall. It was unlocked and he slipped inside, holding the door slightly ajar. The room stank of dirty rags and sour mops. He stood leaning against the door peering out.

At seven o'clock the first girl appeared. She was of medium height, young, and expensively dressed. She rang the bell twice, one long and one short ring. Suddenly the burnished brass door of the peephole snapped open.

Two heavy locks clicked and the door swung open revealing a tall blonde of forty or more. She was astonishingly handsome.

"Come in, Irene," she said. "You're right on time." Her voice was low and cultured.

"Hello, Mildred …." The heavy door swung shut on their conversation.

He heard the heavy locks click into place.

Soon after the first girl entered another fashionably dressed girl appeared and was admitted.

He waited until eight-thirty. By that time six girls had entered the apartment. He made a mental note that they had appeared systematically at fifteen minute intervals.

He took the elevator down. The operator stared at him questioningly but said nothing.

Steve automatically registered the suspicious glances of the operator and doorman. He couldn't enter this building again or they would be screaming cops to Mildred Goldberg. He felt reasonably sure now Mildred was running a highclass whorehouse for tired businessmen. The hours and the location were perfect. The way he had it figured was that the girls arrived early and prepared for the arrival of the 'Johns' sometime after nine in the evening.

He went to the roof of the building behind West End Avenue. It gave a good view of the apartment but the windows were heavily curtained and draped and he could see nothing.

It was almost eleven when he reached home. He glanced up at the house and was surprised to see Rusty's face pressed against the window peering out at him.

He ran up the stairs and into the apartment.

"Rusty," he called, "what's wrong?"

She shrugged and studied him indifferently.

"I was waiting for you," she said, simply. "This old dump is getting under my skin. It's so lonely here I don't know how you stand it."

He kissed her briefly, possessively.

"What's new?" he said.

"What could be new?"

She stared at him sullenly.

"Did you answer any want ads?"

"No," she said, angrily. "Of course not. Today is Tuesday. You know I never go out on Tuesdays."

"Why not?" he teased.

He knew well enough. Tuesday was her bad luck day. It was the day he had arrested her. Wednesday was her good luck day. If the day was cloudy that was an added omen of good luck. Every popular song had a special meaning for her. She found endless excuses for her life and her slackness in the countless symbols of good and evil she lived by. A silver bracelet on her right wrist was luck for the- week. A gold one would bring her harm. Tony had bought her a gold bracelet and two days later had gun whipped her.

"I'll go out tomorrow," she said. "There's a guy I used to work for. Maybe he'll give me a job."

She sounded disinterested and bored with the subject.

"Any mail? Any phone calls?"

"No. Nothing," she said, glaring up at him.

"Any good television programs?" he teased, laughing down into her angry eyes.

She ignored him, taking a cigarette from the pack on the window ledge, she tapped it angrily against her fingernail, placed it between her lips deliberately and lit it.

He ignored the mounting signs of anger.

"Be with you in a minute," he said, going quickly into the bedroom. The bed was unmade and the sheets and bedding were half on the floor.

He hung his jacket in the bedroom closet and was pleased to see all her new summer dresses hanging beside his suits in the closet. He had spent a lot of money on her. Much more than he could afford. But it was worth it. He had never been so happy nor felt so complete in his life.

He made the bed, whistling softly to himself as he did so. He went into the bathroom and washed up. Later, in the kitchen he poured himself a cup of coffee and drank it black. Through the kitchen window he could see, far off, the tiny yellow lights of the apartment houses.

The sink was piled with unwashed dishes and the stove smelled of gas and cold grease. Rusty was awfully good in bed but she didn't know a thing about housekeeping. How could she sit and read cheap magazines and look at television hour after hour when the house was a mess like this? She was forever leaving things uncovered, doors open, and ash trays filled to overflowing. Disorder and untidiness bothered him like a physical ache.

"Rusty," he called.

She didn't answer but he could hear her padding toward the kitchen.

"Are you hungry?" she asked, coming into the kitchen.

"Starving."

"Your supper is in the oven," she said, sitting at the table opposite him.

He removed the hot plate from the oven. It contained a burnt pork chop, some dried up peas and warmed over mashed potatoes.

"Jezus, I can't eat this," he said. "Didn't anyone ever teach you to cook or keep house?"

"No, kid," she said, indifferently. "I'm an orphan, remember?"

"I'm an orphan too," he said. "What the hell has that to do with it?"

She smiled annoyingly at him. Then her eyes became suddenly solemn. "Find out anything about Tony today?" she said.

"No."

She crossed her slender legs, lit a fresh cigarette and rested her chin in her hands.

"Tony used to take me out almost every night."

"Too bad," he said, glaring at her.

"Tony used to treat me real nice," she persisted.

"Tony used to treat me real nice," he mimicked. "Tony used to gun whip me. Tony sent me to the hospital for a month. Tony was a good guy."

Her face became pale and stony eyed. She looked away from him. He had hurt her and he intended to hurt her more. How could she throw Tony up to him like that? "Look," he hissed. "When are you going to get a job?"

"You told me to take it easy until I felt better," she said humbly.

"I didn't tell you to retire," he snapped.

"I'll get a job," she said. "Damn you, I'll get a job tomorrow."

"Good," he said. "I'm glad to hear it."

"And when I do," she said, angrily. "When I do I'll leave this dump so fast ...."

They both knew she was only talking in rancor.

Steve left the kitchen and was back in a moment with his pipe. He sat at the table and lit up, puffing at his pipe thoughtfully.

Suddenly she laughed and her eyes smiled up at him.

"How now, brown cow," she lisped out.

And for no reason they were both laughing. He rose from his chair, lifted her to her feet and hugged her to him, feeling her supple body fit itself into his and then he kissed her hard full on the mouth.

"Look," he said, "are you hungry?"

"I'm starving."

"All right," he said. "Help me clean up this mess and we'll go out and eat somewhere. How's that?"

She pecked at his cheek and smiled at him.

Together they washed the dishes, happy and detached from unpleasant reality in a world of their own strange union.

Later, after the house had been thoroughly cleaned, they both showered and dressed and drove out to a tiny, all night diner near the city's edge.

The next night when he came home Rusty was radiant with excitement.

"Steve," she said, "I got a job today."

"Good," he said, without enthusiasm.

He was surprised at his own reaction. He methodically went around the room emptying ash trays filled with bent and twisted rolls of white paper and tobacco.

"Stop running around cleaning up like an old maid," Rusty said, impatiently.

He sat down, struck a match and lit his pipe and waited. He must accept the fact that Rusty was not his wife and if she wanted to leave him he must agree as gracefully as possible. And yet the thought of marrying a prostitute was so repellent to him he could not consider it. He could live with her, go to bed with her and yet he could not marry her.

"It's a wonderful place, Steve," Rusty's voice cut through his thoughts. "I had a long talk with Mr. Egan. He's the owner and he hired me on the spot."

"That's nice," he said.

He would lose her. His control over her would slip away, and he would miss her like hell if she left him.

"You will like him, Steve."

"I will?" he said. "What the hell is the difference if I like him or not. He hired you, not me."

She fixed her eyes on him questioningly.

"What is the matter with you?"

He tried to smile and relax.

"Nothing." he said. "Tired, I guess. Go ahead, Rusty, I'm listening."

She leaned forward in her chair.

"At first he wasn't sure he would hire me. Said he had two other girls he wanted to interview. But after we talked a little while he changed his mind."

"What made him do that?" he asked, suspiciously.

"Oh," she smiled. "I just talked. I guess he liked my personality."

"I'll bet he did," he said, bitterly, seeing her show off everything she had, letting the man get ideas, right ones probably.

"Hello," she said, snapping her fingers before his eyes. "Are you awake?"

He tried to smile but it turned sour.

"Yeah," he said.

"Forty dollars a week," she went on. "And Mr. Egan says the tips are very good."

"That's nice," he said, staring out the window. "What are the hours?"

"Twelve noon to eight."

"But Rusty," he protested. "In a week I'm due for a new shift. I'll be out from seven until three in the morning. We won't see each other."

"I'll be off Wednesday," she said, indifferently. "You can see me then."

"What's the name of the place?"

"The Blue Lantern Diner."

He knew the spot. It was a new diner located on one of the main arteries leading out of the city. It was a gold mine. Had a good reputation with the police too. Nice, respectable trade, never any trouble there, no drunks, no fights. It was run better than the average diner.

"Nice place," Steve said more encouragingly. "Has a good reputation."

"Mr. Egan's a wonderful man," Rusty said, in a high, excited voice.

He glared at her. "Must you use that voice?"

"Well, he is," she persisted.

"All right, so he's a wonderful man. Must you have an orgasm every time you mention him?"

Suddenly she got the drift and she threw back her head and laughed in the old reckless, inviting way—a white-toothed, open-city kind of a laugh.

"You're jealous?"

"The truth?" he said, frowning at her.

"Yes, the truth."

"You're absolutely right."

And suddenly she was in his arms kissing his face over and over again.

"He's a nice guy, Steve," she said, soothingly. "But he's not you."

"Is that good or bad?"

"Good for you and bad for him."

He held her supple body tight against him.

Gently she disentangled herself.

"This place gives me the creeps," she said, crossing her arms in front of her. "Let's go out somewhere."

They drove far out along the causeway to the beach. He parked the car in the huge cement shelled lot and they walked arm in arm along the esplanade toward the sea. The planked boardwalk was deserted and washed with gray sand from the previous day's cloudburst. The restaurants and pavilions were dark.

They walked in silence through the soft gray sand. Overhead a bright moon lit up the sea with an unearthly luminescence. The beach was empty and the water rushed sideways across the land like an angry crab.

Hand in hand, they stood looking out over the water.

"Steve," she said, in a low voice. "Remember me?"

Her shining red hair blew back clean off her broad forehead. He looked at her and he knew he was going to lose her. It was something as inevitable as the movement of the water in front of them.

"Listen to it," he said.

She shivered and placed her head against his shoulder.

"Don't look like that, Steve," she said.

"How do I look?" he asked, hardly covering his irritability.

"Very sad. As though you don't like being with me."

He lit his pipe and stared out across the water.

"What the hell's the matter with you?" she said, uneasily.

"Are you jealous or something?" she said tenderly.

"When do you start working?" he said.

"Tomorrow."

"That case I told you about will keep me working nights for a couple of weeks."

"Do you have to?"

"Yes," he said.

"Is it Tony?"

"Mildred Goldberg's place. I think there is something there."

"Steve," she said. "That place of yours gives me the creeps at night. I get awful lonely when you're not there."

"What do you want to do about it?" he said, flatly.

This might be it. This might be the exit speech.

"Couldn't we move somewhere else now that I'm working?"

He tried to smile but it got away from him and he grimaced, licking the salt from his lips.

She stroked his face softly. He held her hands and kissed her lightly on the lips.

"Such a gloomy, jealous guy," she said, lovingly.

He pressed his face against her breasts and felt the warm softness of her.

She pushed him away and opened her purse, taking from it a small package.

"He Here," she said, handing it to him.

The package was small and hard and real.

"What is it?"

"Open it," she commanded.

He undid the wrappings. It was a smooth, shiny cigarette lighter with initials engraved on it. It looked expensive. Rusty had no money other than what he gave her to run the household; certainly no money to be buying presents like this.

"It lights in the wind," she said, eagerly.

He flicked the cover up, and a small, yellow-blue flag of flame bent away from the gentle breeze.

She put a cigarette between her lips and he lit it from the small flame. They sat and smoked and stared out at the narrowing horizon.

"Where did you get the money to buy this?"

She was plainly taken aback.

"I saved it from the household money."

"The hell you did."

"But I did, Steve" she protested, tears coming to her eyes.

"The hell you did," he growled again, his whole body shaking with suspicion and jealousy.

"You bastard," she suddenly screamed and pulled away from him. "So goddamned suspicious. All right I didn't save it. I laid for ten guys and I spent it on you. You big stupid jerk. You're nothing but a big, dumb, suspicious cop."

He fondled the smooth lighter, feeling its weight and coolness against the heat of his palm. Suddenly he brought his arm far back and hurled the shiny thing far out into the rushing water.

Rusty put her hands to her eyes and sobbed.

He rose and walked stiffly away from her, torn between feeling sorry and not sorry. But if she didn't follow he would leave her alone on the beach.

"Steve!" she called, running after him. "Steve! Wait!"

He turned and watched her running toward him.

"Steve," she gasped, throwing herself in his arms. "I did save the money. Really, I did, Steve."

He tilted her face to his. "Look," he said, quietly. "I'm going to tell you something."

The large, blue eyes were questioning.

"I want you to get out of my place. Get out of my life and don't ever come back."

"No, Steve," she gasped, "No, Steve."

He dropped to the sand, picking up handfuls of the moist grey stuff and letting it sift through his fingers. He had told her. It was too big for him and he had shifted the burden to her.

"Steve," she pleaded. "I don't want to leave. I want to stay with you." She knelt very close to him and stroked his hair.

He lifted his head and looked at her intently. She forced a smile. There was no loathing, no contempt, no hate—only pleading and love.

He rose abruptly and brushed the sand from his trousers.

"Let's go," he said, abruptly, in a helpless quandary.

He wanted to go where there were people and noise and something to drink. Or he wanted to be alone. But he didn't want to be alone with Rusty.

CHAPTER NINE

THE NEXT DAY Steve's emotions were so confused he felt he had to bury himself in his work. Lieutenant Quinlan, the Vice Squad supervisor, was on vacation so Steve went directly to the Chief.

Chief Rossetti was seated at his desk quietly smoking a large black cigar. In a basket on one side of the desk was a pile of signed reports. The overhead light, which was on constantly day or night, reflected in the Chief's glasses as he puffed clouds of blue cigar smoke across the desk.

As Steve entered the room, the Chief leaned far back on his swivel chair. "Morning, Steve," he said, pleasantly. "What's on your mind?"

The flat eyes under thick glass stared at him absently. The men always considered it a bad sign when the Chief called them by their first names; it generally indicated they were on the way out. Steve dismissed the thought with annoyance. He was getting as bad as Rusty with her silly omens and symbols. The Chief was merely in one of his rare, good moods.

"I've got something I would like to talk over with you, Chief," he said, quietly.

"Pull up a chair."

Steve did as he was told and went immediately into the details of the Mildred Goldberg case.

The Chief listened in that over stimulated way of his.

"Where did you get the lead?" he said, abruptly, as Steve concluded his story.

"From a stoolie." Steve said. He flushed and moved uneasily on the chair.

The Chief rose ponderously from his chair and paced up and down behind the desk blowing clouds of smoke before him.

"I don't like you guys using stoolies," he said.

"How else can we get information, Chief?" Steve said.

"I know you guys have to use stoolies," he said. "But you got to be careful. Stoolies have sent many a good cop to jail."

"I know," Steve said, catching his breath. "But the F.B.I. uses them all the time."

"Sure," the Chief agreed, nodding his big head. "For them it's all right. They even have a special budget item to pay stoolies but for us—no good. Strictly no good. Officially we never use them. In case anybody ever questions you, you never use a stoolie, understand?"

"Yes, sir," Steve said, tearing his eyes away from the Chief's glare.

"All right," the Chief said, flattening out the two lank locks of dyed hair on his bald head. "All right. Now what's on your mind?"

"Well," Steve said, slowly. "We can't go into the building. If she's running a whorehouse, she's got all the building employees on the pad."

"Right," the Chief said, eyeing Steve shrewdly.

"So, I thought, Chief, if you're agreeable, we might assign a policewoman to the case. Get her a job as chambermaid in the building."

"Good idea," the Chief said, quickly. "Damn good idea. Who owns the building?"

"Levy & Sons."

"Who manages it?"

"They do."

"What's their phone number?"

Steve gave it to him.

The Chief called it and made an appointment.

"They'll be up here in half an hour," he said, clumping down the receiver. "Now you want a policewoman, that right?"

"Yes, sir."

The Chief called the Policewoman's Bureau and made arrangements for a policewoman to report to the office immediately.

"Anything else you need, Steve?"

"Yes, sir," Steve said, quickly. "I think we should put a twenty-four hour tap on Mildred Goldberg's telephone."

"Right again," the Chief chuckled, nodding his head.

He pressed the buzzer on his desk and the clerical lieutenant came hurrying into the office.

"Tom," the Chief said, "get up a forty-nine requesting a court order to tap this phone. Possible prostitution."

Steve quickly wrote the number on a piece of scratch paper and handed it to the lieutenant.

"Right, Chief," the lieutenant said, taking the paper. "Anything else?"

"That's all, Tom," the Chief said, dismissing him abruptly.

The Chief got to his feet and paced back and forth nervously behind his desk.

"Steve," he said, turning abruptly to Steve and looking at a spot above his head.

"Yes, sir," Steve said, quickly.

"Did you men attend Bob Sherman's funeral."

"Most of us, yes, sir."

"Were you there, personally?"

"Yes, sir, Jerry and I both went."

The Chief stepped in front of the desk and his open, ruddy face loomed like a grotesque balloon in front of Steve.

"How did he look?"

"Lousy," Steve said. "Didn't look like him at all. They had his face padded out and they had a phony wig on his head. You wouldn't have recognized him, Chief."

"Humph," the Chief snorted. He turned and looked hard into Steve's eyes. "Do you know this is the first time in almost twenty years that I haven't attended the funeral of one of my men."

The commanding officer's attendance at the funeral of one of his men was traditional. However, up to this moment he hadn't realized the Chief regretted not attending this one.

"Were there many flowers?" the Chief asked.

"Yes, sir. The headquarters squad sent a big wreath and his old precinct sent two small ones. Then there were wreaths from all his relatives."

"How did his wife look?"

"Bad," Steve said, flatly. He didn't like remembering her. "She's pregnant, you know."

The Chief nodded.

"How much money did we give her?"

"Well, Ed Hanley gave her the money. I think it was something like fifteen hundred dollars. Bob's old precinct chipped in too."

The Chief nodded again.

"Not much for a woman with four kids and one on the way."

"No, sir."

The Chief lit a fresh cigar and stared through the dirt-grimed window that looked out over a litter filled alleyway.

The policewoman was the first to arrive. She was wearing a smart blue business suit with small, blue cloth covered buttons and a white blouse secured by a single silver clasp at her throat.

She carried the policewoman's black leather bag which held her shield, her gun, a handkerchief, a change purse and mirror.

Her body looked like a fine tool clothed with care for the occasion. Her hair was silky and black but too long for the current style. The low-heeled blue suede shoes she wore gave her long, lithe athletic body a confident, self-assured walk. She seemed self-confidence itself.

The Chief ceremoniously took out a pad of yellow paper and a newly sharpened pencil.

"Sit down," he said, abruptly.

Steve hastily drew up another chair for her.

She smiled pleasantly at him without speaking.

"Let me have your rank, name and shield number," the Chief said, crisply staring down at the paper.

"Policewoman Allison Tillman, Shield 69."

"How long you been on the job?"

"Fourteen months."

"Ever work with plain-clothesmen?"

"No. I've been doing matron duty mostly," she said.

"Yeah." The Chief said, scribbling rapidly on the yellow pad.

The Chief relit his cigar and rose suddenly from the chair. He paced heavily to the window and staring out he spoke to the window letting his voice bounce back into the room. It didn't sound any better that way but talking to this young girl apparently embarrassed him and this was his way of handling the situation.

Patrolwoman Allison Tillman stared askance at Steve, but he only grinned and shrugged his shoulders.

"You'll work with this officer," the Chief intoned solemnly to the window. "Steve Hochuli, Miss Allison Tillman."

It was a stiff, comic way to introduce them and they laughed spontaneously. The Chief turned and stared at them and suddenly he smiled.

"I'm getting old, I guess," he said, half apologetically.

"You'll be assigned with Steve here and his partner. You'll work in close co-operation with them and you will speak to no one regarding this assignment. Is that understood?"

The little speech was delivered in the Chief's best cloak and dagger style. It made Steve smile in spite of himself. The Chief didn't notice. He was staring at the girl.

She kept her eyes fixed on him as she answered quietly. "I understand, sir."

The Chief briefed her quickly on the setup. When he finished he looked at her a long time.

"All that sink in?" he said, ponderously.

"Yes, sir," she said.

"Any questions?"

"No, sir."

"Think you can handle it?"

"Yes, sir."

"Now for the final question," the Chief said, sighing heavily. "Do you want the detail? I don't want to force you into anything you don't want to do. We don't do things that way in this department."

She laughed quietly.

"What are you laughing at?" the Chief snapped.

"I've been searching dead bodies for fourteen months," she explained. "Nobody ever asked me if I like it."

The Chief scowled in anger.

Steve sat aghast. What a naïve thing to say. This kid had a lot to learn about the department mores. She might have spirit but she had better keep it under glass if she wanted to get along with a guy like the Chief.

"Miss Tillman," the Chief snapped. "I don't like your attitude. Everybody in this department takes orders and they don't complain. That's the first thing any cop should learn and, fortunately, most of them do."

He stared fixedly at a spot over her head.

"I'm sorry, sir," she said, flushing. "And I do want the detail."

"That's better."

The clerical lieutenant knocked on the door and poked his head in.

"A Mr. Levy to see you, Chief."

"Send him in."

A tall, well-dressed man walked quietly into the office.

"Get Mr. Levy a chair, Steve," the Chief said, rising to shake hands with the man.

"I'm Chief Rossetti," he introduced himself.

"Sid Levy," the man said, pleasantly.

Steve brought the chair in from the outer office and the man sat expectantly facing the Chief.

After the Chief had put the facts before him the man said, "We'll co-operate fully. Just what do you want us to do?"

"Policewoman Tillman, here," he said, pointing a stubby finger at the girl, "will have to be employed as a chambermaid on that floor. Can you arrange it?"

The man smiled at the girl. "Sure," he said, easily.

"Now another thing," the Chief said, chewing nervously at his cigar. "She'll have to work nights. Say between the hours of seven and three in the morning."

The man pondered a moment before answering. "We have a night chambermaid on that floor," he said, quietly. "However, we'll shift her. The hours are no problem."

"Good," the Chief said, rubbing his hands together. "Now, how soon can she start?"

"Is tomorrow evening convenient?" he asked.

"Fine," the Chief said.

The man wrote quickly on a piece of notebook paper. He handed the scribbled note to the policewoman. "Give this to Mr. Herman, the building manager," he said. "I'll confirm your employment this afternoon." He turned to the Chief. "Her wages will be eight dollars a day. Is that agreeable?"

"Agreed," he said, laughing. "Make the check payable to Miss Tillman just like you would any employee."

"Right," the man said.

"Another thing, Mr. Levy," the Chief cautioned. "Under no circumstances are any of the building employees to know that Miss Tillman is a policewoman."

"Of course," the man agreed.

The man polished his glasses in an embarrassed way.

"Chief," he said, at last. "Our guests at that particular establishment are all fine people—at least we think they are. I shouldn't like any of the others annoyed or embarrassed in any way."

"I understand," the Chief said. "Rest assured, Mr. Levy, we won't make a move until we're absolutely certain of our ground and you can rely on our complete discretion."

"Another point, Chief," the man said, holding his index finger delicately in the air. "We shouldn't care for any undue publicity in the event an arrest."

"We'll do our best," the Chief said. "But we can't promise. We have no control over the press."

The sparring made the policewoman grin at Steve.

"Chief," Steve said, after the man had left, "I think we should hang around when Miss Tillman is working in the building. Just in case she needs us."

The Chief nodded his big head alertly.

"You do that," he said. "I'll cancel your other work until this thing is cleared up."

Steve turned to the girl.

"There's a small restaurant about a block away from the location," he explained, digging into his pocket for his notebook. He scribbled the address and telephone number on a sheet of paper, tore it out and handed it to her. "If you have any trouble or need us just ring up this place. Ask for either Steve or Jerry. Understand?"

"Yes," she said, taking the paper and folding it neatly away in her purse.

"After every tour," the Chief interrupted. "After you finish work, I mean," the Chief corrected himself, "you'll meet Steve here and his partner and give them whatever information you can get."

"I understand," she said, getting up from the chair.

"Just a minute," the Chief said, as she moved to leave. "Any pay you collect from this chambermaid job will be signed over to the city. You're not to cash your checks or spend them. Is that understood?"

"Of course," she said.

"Goodbye, Miss Tillman," the Chief said, rising ponderously. "If I want to speak to you I'll contact you either through Steve here or his partner."

"Yes, sir."

She left, closing the door quietly after her.

"What do you think about her, Steve?" he said, lighting a fresh cigar.

"I think she'll do fine, Chief," he said.

The Chief grunted.

"Well, Chief," he said, rising slowly. "Think I'll get to work. I hope we get this place."

The Chief grunted and stared out the window.

A block east of West End Avenue prosperity ended abruptly. The tenement buildings were held together with sweat and spit. Here there were countless children where childhood did not exist.

Steve sat alone in the dingy little restaurant brooding. The place was ideally suited to brooding. The air was hot and filled with the smell of onions and frying meat and boiling coffee.

He hadn't seen Rusty in two days. She had moved her things from his room and now slept in his grandparents' old brass bed beneath the bleeding heart in its gold gilded frame. He knew she had decided to have nothing further to do with him. It was only a matter of time till she accumulated enough money and moved out on him. He was determined to let her go. The affair was better over and done with though he was reluctant to let her go back to her old life. Yet he had done what he could, he thought to himself, and at the same time he knew he was only rationalizing. He wanted her as desperately as ever.

He brushed absently at the flies that buzzed too close to his coffee. He lifted the thick white mug and drank from it Glancing at his watch he saw it was already seven. Jerry should be showing any minute.

He glanced toward the front of the store where an apoplectic woman in a dirty white apron leaned fatly against the sticky white counter. The red plastic-covered stools tilted at crazy angles on the other side of the counter looking for all the world like a row of drunks hanging over a bar.

It was a dirty little sewer but it was only a block away from the West End Avenue location; it had the advantage of being off the beaten path; and it stayed open all night. For them it was better than a bar because a girl coming in here wouldn't attract attention.

There were only two other tables in the back of the lunchroom. In one an old man wrapped in rags was sleeping. In the other another old man was pretending to read a paper but he was really asleep too.

Steve saw Jerry come in. Jerry sauntered to his table and draped his loose-limbed frame on a chair across from Steve.

"You sure can pick 'em," Jerry said, nodding his lean head at the filthy, fly specked room.

"Got any suggestions?"

"Nope. You're the brains of this operation."

"Thanks."

"By the way, I've been over to the wiretap."

"Yes?"

"Nothing. Not a peep out of the phone all day."

Steve frowned. "Where's the tap located?" he said slowly.

"Ed Manley found a bridge in the backyard and they backstrapped it into an empty store. The super thinks they're narcotics men.

Then neither spoke as the fat, apoplectic woman waddled to the table.

"Damned truck broke down again," Jerry said as the waitress stood bored and disinterested at the table.

"I tell you, I'm going to quit this job if he don't get us—"

"You want something?" the waitress interrupted.

Jerry glanced up with surprise. "Oh, hello, Beautiful," he said. "How's business?"

"What you want?" Her voice was flat and bored.

"Coffee."

"That all, coffee?"

"Yeah, coffee and a piece of pie."

"What kind?" .

"Apple."

"We ain't got apple."

"What have you got?"

The waitress' weak eyes gleamed in triumph.

"Pineapple-cheese."

"I'll take it and clean the fly-dirt off."

When the waitress left Jerry turned in disgust to Steve.

"What a blister that is," he said.

Steve grinned, enjoying Jerry's annoyance.

They spoke in desultory fashion for a little while and then lapsed into silence.

At about eleven o'clock Jerry yawned loudly.

"Steve," he said, suddenly. "No point in both of us hanging around. Think I'll go over and see how the boys are making out on the tap."

"Go ahead," Steve said, indifferently. "Bring me a paper when you come back."

Steve ordered more coffee and a sandwich. He lit his pipe and put his feet on a chair. Leaning back against the wall he smoked his pipe, blowing clouds of smoke at the swarms of flies that hovered busily over the table. The flies circled away and came back when the smoke cleared. The telephone hadn't rung once since he had been there.

Jerry appeared again about twelve o'clock and slapped the newspaper down on the table.

"Anything doing on the tap?"

Jerry jabbed at a fly and missed.

"Not a thing," he said. "A real stiff."

At two o'clock Jerry left again to get a shot at the bar on the corner. He had hardly gone out when the policewoman showed.

She glanced uncertainly through the open doorway into the lunchroom and then, seeing him in the back, she walked slowly to the rear of the place.

"Hot, isn't it," she said, petting her hair into place in an embarrassed way.

"Yeah," he said, half rising." Have a seat."

She ordered iced tea from the fat waitress and sat sipping it through a straw.

"Boy, this tastes good," she said.

He nodded and puffed thoughtfully at his pipe. He waited patiently for her to talk.

"How did it go tonight?" he said, at last.

"Terrible," she said, holding up her hands. "Look at these hands."

They were very red.

"Strong soap?" he said.

"Acid soap," she said, sipping at the tea. "I worked like a dog all night."

"Find out anything?" he said, abruptly.

"A little," she said.

"What?"

"Mildred Goldberg is on vacation in Atlantic City."

"Anything else?"

"She just had the apartment redecorated.

He nodded.

"Any idea when she'll be back?"

"Tomorrow morning."

"Good," he said. "She'll probably have the girls in tomorrow."

The girl wet her full red lips.

"All right if I call you Steve? You can call me Ally."

"Agreed," he said, smiling at her.

"Steve," she said, lighting a cigarette, "there's a funny atmosphere about that place?"

"What do you mean?" he said, quickly.

"It's hard to put your finger on," she said, hesitantly. "It's a feeling you get as though it was a closed corporation or something. The doorman and the elevator man are talking but when they see me they stop and move away. And the way they look at me, as though I was a strange animal of some kind."

"Could be you're only imagining it," he said, neutrally.

"No, I'm not," she persisted. "The same thing happened with the night clerk and the manager. They treated me like dirt."

"Could mean one of two things," he said, quietly.

"I'm listening," she said.

"Well, either they made you as a policewoman or, what is more likely, it's because you are a stranger and they don't know or trust you yet."

She smiled pleasantly in agreement.

"Makes sense," she said. "About the only one who was at all friendly was the chambermaid who had the floor before I came. Her name is Lucy. She's the one who gave me the information about Mildred Goldberg."

Steve tamped fresh tobacco into his pipe and lit it.

"Of course," he said, "if there is something going on in the building like we suspect, they'll all be closer than thieves."

Jerry came ambling up to the table.

"Jerry," Steve said, introducing them, "Ally Tillman, the Policewoman assigned to work with us on this case."

"Hi, Beautiful," Jerry said, casually.

"Is that how you always greet girls?" she retorted, with genuine annoyance.

Jerry was plainly surprised. He shot a glance at Steve.

"Take it easy," Jerry said, soothingly. "Don't get your back up. No offense."

She ignored Jerry and turned to Steve. "I'm dead," she said peevishly. "And I live in Brooklyn."

Steve and Jerry exchanged sick glances.

"Well, Steve, old boy," Jerry said, quickly, "I've got to beat it. See you both tomorrow night."

He left without looking at the policewoman.

"Is he always that way?" she said, staring after Jerry.

"Oh, you'll get used to him," Steve said, rising slowly. "Tell you what—I'll drive you home."

She smiled at him gratefully.

On the way home she talked incessantly. She had been born and raised in the Williamsburg section of Brooklyn. Her father was dead and she was the sole support of her mother. She had a married brother and sister who had run away and left her at home stuck with her mother. She was studying to be a lawyer at night school and she was glad the semester was ended, especially since she had this detail.

Steve was glad to say goodnight to her. The girl had extraordinary talent for feeling sorry for herself—especially for a policewoman.

Steve watched her open the bedroom door and peek in. He squinted guardedly at her and then turned over on his side facing the window. The dark shades were down but the bright afternoon sun filtered around the sides of the window frames in bright, thin rays.

The slight rustle of her dress and the muted ticking of the clock were the only sounds in the quiet room.

He felt her staring down at him. He felt the bottom corner of the bed give as she sat on it. He knew he looked like a slob. Last night he had come home dead, fallen into bed fully clothed. His collar was open and his tie dangled from his jacket pocket. His pants were wrinkled and his face was dirtied by a thirty-six hour beard. His head was foggy and he needed a shower.

She sniffled a little and the tears started. At first it was only a low sob and then it got too loud to ignore. He knew how she felt. Their life together was like a forgotten child's top that had stopped spinning.

He sighed and turned over and sat up, rubbing his knuckles against his closed eyelids.

"What's the matter?" he said but without sympathy.

"Oooh," she sobbed. "I'm so lonely."

He glanced at the time. It was four o'clock.

"What are doing home?" he said.

"It's my day off," she said, brushing at her eyes with a handkerchief.

"Why don't you go to a movie," he suggested.

"I don't want to go to a movie," she pouted.

"What do you want?"

"I'm lonely," she sobbed. "I'm awful lonely."

"I get the idea," he snapped. "All right get undressed and come to bed."

"Ohh, you bastard," she cried. "You great big dumb bastard."

He waited.

"One of these days I'm going to walk out on you. You just wait. I'll leave you flat."

He tried to put his arms about her but she jumped quickly up from the bed.

"I'm sorry, Rusty," he apologized. "I'm half asleep and don't know what I'm saying."

"You know all right," she said, accusingly.

"Look," he said, lighting a cigarette. "What can I say?"

She bared her small white teeth like a vixen ready to bite.

"Big deal," she said, and then mimicking him, "All right get undressed and come to bed. I tell you I'm lonely and that's what you say."

"Think it's a bad idea?" he sneered to cover his guilty conscience.

"Oooh," she cried bitterly. "I'll fix you. I'll fix you."

She ran from the room, slamming the door behind her before he fully realized what had happened. He fell back on the bed, already half-asleep again.

By seven Steve sat alone in the dirty little restaurant, reading the evening paper and sipping his coffee, trying not to think of Rusty. He was giving her quite a beating but he couldn't help it. He didn't want her around any more and he hoped she would leave him. She was becoming an hysterical nuisance. The less he saw of her the better. But supposing she should leave; would he go chasing after her as he had done before? He felt very sorry for her. You could see her thoughts, her hunger and hatred all stuck to her eyeballs. But she cost so much in everything but money—even that.

"Hey, wake up," Jerry said, sitting down at the table.

Steve glanced up, startled. He hadn't even seen Jerry enter the place.

"Some cop," Jerry derided him. "A guy could walk right up and rob him and he wouldn't know it."

"I was day dreaming I guess," Steve said, rubbing his eyes.

"The wiretap is red hot," Jerry said. "Apparently been going all day."

"Anything good?" Steve said, excitedly.

"All good," Jerry said, nodding in a knowing way."Our little pigeon has been calling up her girls and telling them to be at the apartment on time—the vacation is over."

"Sounds promising," he said, doubtfully. "That all they got?"

Jerry made no attempt to conceal his annoyance.

"No," he said, shortly, "they got the works. She contacted some oil company and told them she has seven new girls. Seems they have a sales convention in town. They're fixing up their seven top sales representatives."

Steve breathed a deep sigh of relief.

"That should wrap it up all right," he said.

"Worried, eh, kid?" Jerry said, staring at him intently.

"Sure," he said. "You would be too in my position. If this thing flubbed, the Chief would drop me like a hot potato."

Jerry nodded his slim head in agreement and sucked on a toothpick he had in the comer of his mouth.

"He's like that all right," he said.

Steve rose suddenly and put his jacket on.

"Hold the fort will you, Jerry," he said. "I'm going out for a shot."

"Celebrating already?" Jerry said, grinning mockingly at him.

"No," Steve said. "I just need a shot for my morale."

"You look like you could use a shot all right," Jerry goaded him. "What's the matter? Didn't you get any sleep?"

He decided that lots of people must find Jerry hard to get along with. It must have taken years to work all those irritating ways to such a fine edge.

He tossed the newspaper to Jerry. "Read and get educated," he said.

"Yeah," Jerry said.

He walked quickly the two short blocks to the bar. He sat at the end of the bar near the window. A big silver fan in the corner was circulating the stale air and a group of elderly men and women at the opposite end of the bar conversed in whispers. A wizened Japanese bartender came over and placed a bowl of pretzels in front of him.

"Rye and soda," Steve said.

He had three shots and left, the whisky warming his stomach and giving him a pleasant glow. When he got back to the lunchroom Jerry had news for him.

"The policewoman just phoned," he said, rapidly. "The place is loading up. Five women and four 'Johns' are in already."

"We had better get the Chief down here," Steve said.

He called the Chief at his home.

"Yeah?" the Chief answered the phone.

"Steve Hochuli, Chief," he said, quickly. "The place is going."

"All right," the Chief said, instantly awake. "Give me the address of where you are."

Steve could hear him groping around for a pencil and paper.

"Ready, Chief?" he said.

"Go ahead."

Steve gave him the address.

"Now," the Chief's voice came over the wire sharp and crisp. "Contact the clerical man at the office. Have him phone the entire squad. Give him the address of the lunchroom and have them meet you there and wait for me."

"Yes, sir," Steve said.

"Oh, yeah," the Chief said. "Another thing. Tell the clerical man to have one of the men pick up that sledgehammer at the office. Get that?"

"Yes, sir."

"All right. I'll be down there in half an hour. Have the clerical man tell the others to get there fast as they can."

"Yes, sir."

The telephone clicked.

Within twenty minutes the entire squad was assembled in the sleepy little lunchroom, mulling around, shouting humorless jokes to one another in the overstimulated air—their faces still swollen with sleep. They drank cup after cup of coffee to help them wake up.

The Chief showed right on the half hour. The open, ruddy face was alive with excitement. You would have sworn this was the very first raid he had ever been on. He looked like a thick set businessman in his gray striped business suit and gray homburg.

"All right men," he said, sitting at one of the three tables in the rear of the lunchroom and taking charge. "This is going to be a raid on a whorehouse."

The men gathered in a semi-circle around the table still drinking from the hot mugs of coffee.

"Have they all got the location, Steve?" he looked up and asked.

"Yes, Chief," Steve said next to him.

"All right. How many cars have we got?"

"Eight cars, Chief," somebody volunteered.

"We don't want that many," the Chief said, stuffing a fat black cigar into his mouth and lighting it. "Put six men in a car. Two cars are all we need."

"Chief," Steve said, "there's a small alleyway about four buildings down from the location. Maybe half of us could sneak through it and go up the rear fire-escape and break in that way."

The Chief glanced thoughtfully at Steve.

"Think that's the best way?" he said, doubtfully.

"I think so, Chief," Steve said, promptly. "She's got the front door double-locked from the inside and even if we did get the key from the night clerk I doubt if it would do any good. We'd have to crash the place anyway. If we got in through the fire-escape we could open the door for the others."

The Chief snapped his thick fingers.

"Anybody pick up the sledgehammer at the office?" he said.

"Got it in my car, Chief," one of the men called from the rear of the group.

The Chief puffed hard at his cigar and glanced at the men.

"Any other suggestions?" he said.

"Let's go, Chief," one of the men shouted excitedly.

"All right men," he said. "Half go with Steve and the other half with me."

"We have our men picked out, Chief," Jerry spoke up.

"Good," the Chief agreed. "All six of you use one car." He glanced at his watch. "It's three-fifteen now," he said. "We'll give you fifteen minutes to get into the alley and up the fire-escape."

He turned to the other half of the squad gathered around him. "Everybody understand that? We'll be at the front door of her apartment at exactly three-thirty. Think that'll be enough time?"

"That should do it, Chief," Steve said.

"Now when you get in there," the Chief instructed, "one man stay at the window so nobody gets out. Another man heads straight for the front door to let us in. You, Steve, you know what the madam looks like?"

"Yes, Chief."

"All right, see if you can grab her first. She'll try to get rid of the records. Get her before she does."

"Yes, sir."

"Now, the rest of you guys locate the bedrooms and see that the girls and the 'Johns' stay in the rooms. Don't let anybody move until I get in there. Everybody understand?"

There was a chorus of, "Yes, Chief."

The men exited quickly from the tiny lunchroom and got into the parked cars.

Six men squeezed into Jerry's car, groaning with discomfort as they sat down.

"Let's get this over with," Ed Manley said. "I'm being crushed to death."

"Stop just after you turn the corner," Steve instructed. "The alleyway is right there."

"Hope there's no uniformed men around," Bill said, fretfully, "or we're liable to end up with bullets in our cans for our trouble."

The six men padded through the alleyway, playing their flashlights on shadowy objects that stood in their way. They emerged into the unbroken night shadows and stopped beside the massive building whose forbidding walls plunged straight upward. The skeleton form of the fire-escape clung tenaciously to its straight walls. Overhead pale stars shone occasionally through the low, scudding clouds.

Jerry catapulted into the air and clutched the lowest rung of the rusty ladder that led to the fire-escape. It gave a brief, shrill screech like a nail being pulled from a board. They held their breaths and stood perfectly still and silent. No movement nor sound came from the first floor apartment. In a moment Jerry unhooked the ladder and slid it quietly down to the waiting hands below. One by one they climbed silently up the fire-escape past the first three floors, stifling their harsh breathing and licking their dry lips. The shades of the first three floors were drawn and the windows closed. On the third floor a bedroom light still glowed but it was only a tiny red night light.

Steve followed Jerry to the fourth level of the fire-escape and stood beside him as he tried to force the window open. The other four men were strung out on the landing and along the ladder connecting the two levels.

From far off they heard the mournful scream of a train whistle and they froze. In a moment Jerry was back working on the window with his penknife. At last there was a small snapping sound and the window lock was forced.

Inch by inch Jerry lifted the window and then he cursed softly.

"There's a screen," he whispered to Steve.

Steve held his finger to his lips for silence.

Jerry slipped the sharp point of the penknife into the screen and there was a sharp rasping sound as he cut away on it.

"Who's that?" a frightened girl's voice called out, as they crashed through the screen into the room.

The light went on. A slender, young dark haired girl was standing naked beside the bed clutching a silken nightgown over her breasts.

A middle-aged, bald headed man was sitting upright on the bed, an unlit stump of cigar in his mouth, his hairy chest sprinkled with gray cigar ash. The room gave off a strong odor of liquor and expensive perfume.

"What is it?" the man asked in a husky, frightened voice.

"Police," Steve announced. "Get up out of there and put your clothes on."

The plain-clothesmen came pouring into the room through the window.

"Bill, you stay here at the window," Steve directed.

He led the way, switching on lights as they entered each new room. At last they hurried through a wide, high corridor into a large living room that smelled of fresh paint.

Another corridor led from the living room and the men rushed along it opening the bedroom doors and awakening the occupants.

A heavy sledgehammer crashed against the front door of the apartment and pandemonium broke loose as naked, pudgy, middle aged men holding bundles of clothing in their arms and slim, naked young girls, shrieking hysterically, ran from the bedrooms, with the plain-clothesmen in close pursuit.

Steve raced along the corridor and opened the front door.

"What the hell took you so long?" the Chief shouted, brushing past the plain-clothesman with the sledgehammer.

"Just got in, Chief," Steve explained, quickly. "There was a screen on the window."

"Did you get the madam?"

"Not yet."

"Well, *get her!*" the Chief roared angrily. "She'll be destroying the records and we need them. Get her."

Steve wheeled and ran to the other end of the corridor. He opened a small door that led to a combination bedroom and office.

There was an adjoining toilet and he could hear the bowl flushing. He tried the door but it was locked. He hurled his weight against the door and it gave way with a sickening crash and splintering of wood.

The tall, blonde woman was there, her handsome face reflecting both anger and fear. Her great bosom rose and fell in agitation. She was fully dressed and in her large hands she held the remains of a small black book. He grabbed it from her. In the toilet bowl were small bits of paper going round and round in the water below.

He glanced at the remains of the black book. The second half of it was intact.

"Get out of here," he ordered the woman.

She glared defiantly at him.

"Who the hell are you?"

The cultured tones he had heard weeks earlier had only been a façade. Now they were down to bedrock.

"Police," he said, slipping the book into his pocket as Jerry came rushing in.

"What you got, Steve?"

"Meet Mildred Goldberg. Take her m with the rest."

Jerry grabbed her arm into a half-nelson and hurried her along the corridor as she protested vehemently.

Steve made a systematic search of the desk in the small room. He threw the covers off the bed and lifted the mattress. Nothing. He searched the clothes in the closet and tapped the desk and floors for hidden drawers and loose boards. Nothing. Only what was left of the black book in his pocket.

He thumbed through the book with its endless listings of names and telephone numbers. Under S was the name, Tony Suraci, and his telephone number. Steve quickly copied it into his own notebook. At last he had a direct lead on the guy.

The Chief came charging into the room, the policewoman following him. Her face was flushed and her eyes reflected the Chief's excitement. He hardly recognized her in her cleaning woman's uniform.

"What have you got, Steve?"

Steve handed him the remains of the black book.

"That's all?" he roared, shaking the book at Steve.

"That's all," Steve said quietly. "She flushed the rest down the toilet."

The Chief glowered.

"Thought we would get more than this."

"Look in it, Chief," Steve said. "It's loaded with names and telephone numbers. Should keep us busy for months."

The Chief thumbed through the book with his thick fingers. At last he nodded his head. He glanced around suddenly. "Where is the madam?" he shouted.

They went outside together to where the men and girls were lined up in the living room all in various stages of undress and all trying desperately to get into their clothing.

The girls, frightened and white-faced, were huddled in a far corner of the room with the madam, who glared contemptuously at the police.

"Where's the madam," the Chief whispered to Steve.

He pointed her out and as they glanced at her she shouted, "What are you waiting for? Why don't you lock us up?"

The Chief glanced at her thoughtfully through his glasses, his bland face revealing nothing. He turned to the policewoman at his side.

"Take her back into her room and search her," he said quietly.

As the policewoman attempted to escort the madam out of the room she began to scream.

"I want a lawyer. Nobody's going to search me. I want a lawyer."

"Steve," the Chief grunted. "Help get her back to her room and wait outside while she's being searched."

Steve assisted the policewoman in half dragging, half carrying the big protesting, screaming, biting woman back to her room. He stood outside the door, nursing the fleshy part of his hand where the woman had bitten him, as the policewoman searched her.

At last the policewoman emerged from the room, disheveled and angry.

"Find anything?" Steve said.

"Nothing," the policewoman replied disgustedly. "And, believe me, she was some bitch to search. Wouldn't stand still a minute."

"Tell her to get dressed."

In a few minutes the policewoman and the madam emerged from the little room. The madam was fully and carefully dressed and protesting vigorously as they led her, red faced with anger, back to the Chief.

"I'll have your job," she screamed at the Chief, her eyes blazing with fury. "I want a lawyer." She turned to her girls. "Don't any of you girls talk to these bums until we get a lawyer," she screamed.

"If you don't keep quiet," the Chief warned, "we'll take means to shut you up."

His eyes were hard as rock and there was no anger but a grim determination in his voice.

The woman, who was half a head taller than he, glanced contemptuously at him but remained silent.

"Policewoman find anything on her?" he whispered to Steve.

Steve shook his head negatively. "Not a thing, Chief."

"She's been in this business a long time," the Chief said, glancing at the woman knowingly.

"I checked the files," Steve said, quickly. "There's no record on her, at least not under the name of Mildred Goldberg."

"Could be a phony."

Steve nodded.

The cries of the 'Johns' were heard everywhere now.

"Officer, officer, please listen to me! I'm a married man with two children. My wife—my marriage won't stand this."

"Officer, please let me go. I'll give you everything I have." Wallets and money were flashed.

"Here, here take it. There's six hundred bucks. It's yours. Only let me go."

And invariably, the growling, annoyed reply.

"Talk to the Chief."

Finally the Chief's bellowing voice drowned out the lesser voices in the room.

"Everybody shut up," he shouted, glaring around angrily and chewing on a fresh cigar, his gray Homburg pushed far back on his bald, perspiring head. "Now, listen to me! If I hear anyone, and I mean anyone, offer one of my men a bribe, I'll lock you up for bribery, and if you think I'm kidding, try me out."

The 'Johns' looked at each other and fell silent, terrified worry still on their faces.

"What are you waiting for?" the madam suddenly shouted at the Chief.

He glanced at her thoughtfully.

"The D.A.," he replied, mildly.

In a remarkably short time an assistant District Attorney appeared on the scene, accompanied by a sleepy looking stenographer and reporters and photographers from every paper in the city.

The reporters and photographers crowded into the room, taking pictures and asking questions, while the men and weeping girls attempted to hide their faces beneath hats, coats and dresses.

"Do you want these reporters in here?" the Chief asked the handsome, dapper, assistant D.A.

The young man's voice was soft, liquid and assured when he answered rhetorically and loud enough for all to hear.

"Of course, Chief. Freedom of the press is one of our most sacred traditions."

The young assistant D.A. obediently doffed his hat for the photographers who were taking his picture as he made his little speech.

The Chief grunted in disgust and got down to business.

"That one over there," he said, pointing a thick finger, "is the madam. Name is Mildred Goldberg. Probably a phony."

The young man nodded and smiled politely, turning his handsome profile to a photographer who was snapping his picture.

"Where can we set up shop, Chief?"

They directed him to the little room where Mildred Goldberg had her office. Once the stenographer had set up his little stenotype machine on its thin tripod, the assistant D.A. began calling witnesses.

One by one each of the fifteen people who had been in the apartment at the time of the raid was called in and interviewed, his statement being duly recorded.

It took four hours and the sun was already high when the testimonies were completed. The 'Johns,' without exception, agreed to co-operate fully in the probe and prosecution of the prostitutes and their madam and, after being assured their names would be withheld by mutual agreement among the newspapermen, they were permitted to leave. The 'Johns' refused to talk to the reporters who hounded them on the way out and did their best to prevent their pictures being taken.

The patrol wagons were called and the women bundled off to the local precinct for search and record.

As they were leaving the premises the Chief announced that each man who had been on the raid would have the next tour off.

Later in the headquarters office, the Chief called Steve to one side.

The Chief's eyes smiled at Steve through his thick-lensed glasses.

"I'm putting you and Jerry in for the additional two hundred and fifty a year raise," he said.

Steve smiled his pleasure. "Thanks, Chief," he said, huskily.

"All right," the Chief said. "Go on home now and get some sleep. You look pooped."

As Steve drove toward home he felt he was the happiest man in the world. He was grateful to everybody. He loved everyone. The Chief, for the raise, Rusty for the information and the other plain-clothesmen for being such great, cooperative guys. He would make up to Rusty for the shabby way he had been treating her. Well, now with a little time off and no more night work for awhile they would be seeing more of each other.

CHAPTER TEN

S TEVE SQUINTED as he stepped into the sunlight. Riffled waves of heat simmered up from the roof of the house. In the bright sunlight it looked tall and gray and lonely.

He walked slowly up the carpeted stairs to his apartment. The place looked dirtier and gloomier than ever. He glanced into his grandparents' room which was Rusty's room now. Her blue nightgown was tossed across the unmade bed and there were old newspapers and magazines strewn along the floor. Her dresser was a mess of spilled powder and opened jars of cold cream and lipstick. The two ashtrays on the little night table were filled with crumbled, half-smoked cigarettes.

He went into his room. He drew the dark shade, undressed and tumbled into bed, asleep before his head touched the pillow.

His sleep was unsettling and filled with violent nightmares. He climbed up through the muddy layers of sleep to wakefulness. He was covered with perspiration. He glanced at his watch. It was four o'clock. He had slept for six hours. Rusty wasn't due home for another three hours.

He lay on his bed with his arms folded beneath his head. The window was open and the shade flapped suddenly as a warm, sweet breeze filled the room. He could hear the rush of automobiles past the house and the occasional clack of footsteps on the slate pavement in back of the house.

He felt listless and dull now that the pressure was off. It was easy to understand why ulcers were considered an occupational disease among the police. The continual tension, the night work, the sudden spurts of frantic activity and then the tapering off only to have the whole process repeated, to the endless seasoning of coffee, strong and black, as soon as the next case presented itself.

On a sudden impulse he rose from the bed. He went to the bathroom, shaved, showered and put on a fresh suit of clothes.

Outside he got the car out and drove swiftly away from the house.

Part of the sky was still light and off in the distance, past the empty lots and the elevated, the wooden houses seemed to be leaning against the twilight sky.

A brightly lighted bus rattled out of the semi-darkness, and he swung easily into the outside lane away from it. He parked the car on a cobble stoned street and went across to where a blue and white show window was filled with cigarette lighters, stainless frying pans and tubes of toothpaste. An electric sign, held in place by rusty struts, announced: DRUG STORE & LUNCHEONETTE.

He went in and ordered two hamburgers, without onions, and coffee. Rusty didn't like the smell of onions on his breath.

"How's it coming, Steve?" Max, the bald headed pharmacist asked.

He had known Max for a long time. Used to buy ice cream sodas here when he was a kid. It was a special treat he gave himself as a reward for going to the dentist.

The counterman shoved a plate with two hamburgers in front of him and slapped the coffee down beside it.

"Still a bachelor, Steve?" Max inquired.

"Yeah," he said, munching the hot sandwich.

He hadn't been here since before the war and Max spoke to him as though he had never been away.

After he finished eating he bought two new handkerchiefs. Rusty had forgotten to send the wash out and there were no clean handkerchiefs at home. He placed one in his trouser pocket and fitted the other into his jacket. The little man watched him as he fumbled to separate the handkerchief into three points in the pocket.

"You look like a real sheik. Heavy date?"

"Yeah," Steve grinned.

He was amused to find his reactions were still those of a shy little boy when he talked with Max.

"You should be getting married soon."

"Be seeing you, Max," Steve said, going to the door.

He sat through a silly cowboy feature at the movies and glanced at his watch. Nine o'clock. Rusty should be home by now. He was surprised at his excitement. A couple of weeks was a long time not to have anything to do with a girl like Rusty. You missed her in spite of yourself. Besides, she was responsible for the increase in pay he was getting and that good pinch on West End Avenue.

He stopped at a florist's and bought her six long-stemmed roses. The florist wrapped them in gay green paper and winked broadly at him when he paid for them.

As he entered the apartment he heard small rhythmic sounds coming from Rusty's room and then suddenly the sounds were cut off sharp leaving a vacuum of strained silence.

He switched the light on in Rusty's room.

There was a man in bed with her.

"What are you doing home?" Rusty giggled.

There was no fear or surprise in her voice. It seemed almost as though she had hoped this would happen. She had planned it.

An odd thing was happening to him. Instinctively he had known that one day he would come home to this.

"Come on. Up and out!" he heard his own voice; a policeman's harsh, commanding voice.

The man in bed beside her was a pitiable object. The light caught his frightened face. It was an emaciated face with damp locks of hair sticking in wisps to his brow.

"Move!" he rasped at the man.

The man's limbs, when he rose from the bed, were thin and slack as though broken at the joints.

"Listen, fellow," he said, haltingly.

"Shut up and get dressed," Steve said, leaning against the doorway.

Rusty sat up in the bed, gathering her clothes from the night table beside the bed. She began dressing deliberately, yawning now and then without looking at him.

He studied her with clinical interest.

"Get a move on," he said, in a low voice.

Rusty's blue eyes filled with wicked light.

"What are you going to do, Steve?" she said, sweetly. She covered her mouth daintily as she yawned.

"I hardly even know her," the man was protesting feebly, as he pulled on his trousers.

"Save it, sucker," Steve snapped at him.

Rusty bared her teeth like a vixen ready to bite.

"Always picking on people who can't fight back. The brave hero!"

Automatically she smoothed her dress at the hips with her small, nervous hands.

Steve strode over to the closet and pulled the two new suitcases he had bought her down from the top shelf. He tossed them heavily to the floor in front of them.

"Pack," he said.

Her countenance was contorted with malevolence. Her hands trembled violently as she gathered her things together.

"You help her," Steve said, directing the man to the bureau where Rusty had started pulling her things out of the drawers.

She pressed herself intimately against the man with assumed ardor.

"Don't pay any attention to him," she said, kissing him violently on the lips.

"No, please don't," the man protested feebly, starting back in horror.

Dressed, he was a tall, thin, neatly dressed man in a light summer suit. He was in his late forties, not more, and he stood very straight. His hair was still black and curled crisply against his narrow head, though there was gray at the temples. His mouth was small and pale, his movements quick and nervous like those of a cat. The man was overcome with fear. Here was a man who could be pushed right out of the world, so great was his fear.

"Hurry it up," Steve said, quietly.

Rusty ran to him suddenly and before he could stop her she reached up and placed her arms around his neck and kissed him full on the lips.

"Give me a break, Steve," she said, breathlessly. "It's been weeks since you even looked at me. It was your fault, Steve. It was your fault."

He pushed her roughly away from him.

"You're going with him," he said, grimly.

"Please, Steve. I don't even know the guy. He's just someone I picked up. This is the first time with him—honest."

"Sure," Steve said, the clinical look of detached interest back on his face again.

A dull flush spread over her face and neck.

"I left a new pair of shoes in your room. Can I get them?"

"Sure. Go ahead," he said, easily, glad she was being cooperative.

He watched her as she entered his room.

"Look, fellow," the man said, timidly, diverting his attention back to the room. "She doesn't want to go with me. Why don't you let her stay? I have two hundred dollars I'll give you to forget everything."

Steve examined the man curiously.

"You think this is a shake?"

"No, no," the man protested weakly. "Nothing like that."

"She goes with you."

"Steve!"

It was Rusty's voice coming from the doorway. There was a note in it he had never heard before. He swung around.

She stood there in the doorway, his big service revolver balanced in her trembling hands. Even as she stared at him those enormous blue eyes were drifting out of focus.

"Put it down, Rusty," he said, not moving.

The gun looked big and awkward and strange in her hands. His service revolver that he had hidden away under a pile of shirts in the second drawer of his bureau. His Smith & Wesson .38 Special. The gun he didn't use in plain-clothes because it was too big and unwieldy for the work.

The muzzle was pointed at the spot between his eyes. She had cocked the hammer and her finger was touching nervously on the trigger. Her face was convulsed, her lips drawn back over her small, white teeth.

"Don't be foolish, young lady," the man behind Steve said, unexpectedly and with a quiet dignity. "Come home with me. I want you to. Do you hear?"

She stared at the man, her eyes opening and closing, opening and closing. Slowly they lost their bright intensity. Her face went white and vacant. She began to tremble.

Steve moved toward her quickly. The gun dropped from her limp hands into his. He uncocked the trigger cautiously and slipped the gun into his belt.

"You throw me out and I'll have your shield," she said. Her voice was almost languid.

"Sure," he said.

"You don't believe me?"

"Get the hell out of here," he said. "Do what you want."

"You're serious then," she said.

"Yeah. All the time."

He watched the man gather up the valises and follow Rusty to the door. He listened as their footsteps faded down the stairs. At last the door slammed and they were gone. He stumbled into the living room and sank into the deep, old sofa. He cupped his face in his hands and gritted his teeth to keep from crying.

Next morning, when Steve arrived for work, the office was alive with excitement and tension.

The buzzer sounded and Lieutenant Quinlan called above the hubbub, "All right men, everybody into the Chief's office for a line-up."

Steve was the last man to file into the office. He found a place against the wall.

Seated next to the D.A., who was in a huddle with the Chief, was Rusty. She was heavily made up. She wore a tight fitting green skirt that had slipped above her crossed knees and a white satin blouse opened to her breast. She looked exactly what she was—a whore. She spotted him the minute he entered the office. Her blue eyes were blank as she gazed obstinately at the wall away from him.

The Chief, red faced with anger, spoke in a subdued voice to the D.A., a tall, important looking man with a round head and lightless blue eyes.

The Chief glanced up and glowered at the men.

"They all here, Lieutenant?"

"Yes, sir," Quinlan responded quickly.

"All right, pick him out, Miss," he said to Rusty.

"That's him," she said, pointing to Steve. "The man standing in the corner next to the wall."

Her voice was loud and vindictive.

"Go over and put your hand on his shoulder so there's no mistake."

The men stiffened as Rusty rose and walked toward them. She looked very small against the tall men standing before her. They stepped aside as she walked through the first row to Steve.

She almost smiled as she touched him. He felt the blood from his face and cold beads of perspiration break out on his forehead.

"All right, Miss," the Chief said.

He turned to the D.A. "You want to question him?"

The D.A. glanced briefly at Steve with his lightless blue eyes. He shook his head slowly. "No, Chief," he said, quietly. "I'll leave it in your hands."

The D.A. pushed some papers into his expensive briefcase, shook hands solemnly with the Chief and ushered Rusty quickly out of the room.

Silence, hard and unyielding as rock, encompassed the room as the door closed on their retreating figures.

The Chief's booming voice split through the quiet.

"I told you men again and again not to get mixed up with prosts—but you don't listen."

He stuffed a large cigar into his mouth and chewed on it angrily.

"Hochuli, come up here and sit down."

Steve stumbled forward on wooden legs. The strange sensation of falling was more acute now. He settled clumsily into the chair.

A stenographer, book in hand, hurried into the room.

The Chief pulled the small, green book of department rules and regulations from his desk. He thumbed through it and finally placed the open book before Steve.

"Read the underlined words out loud," he directed.

From far away Steve heard his voice saying, "A member of the department found guilty of making a false official statement may be dismissed from the department."

The Chief closed the book and threw it back into the drawer.

"Understand what that means, Hochuli?"

"Yes, sir."

The Chief cleared his throat and nodded to the stenographer to begin taking notes.

"Do you know that prost who was in here?"

"Yes, sir."

"Did she ever live with you?"

"Yes, sir."

"How long?"

"Three months."

"You knew she was a prost."

"Yes, sir."

"Did you have sex relations with her?"

"Yes, sir."

Steve stared at the floor. Rock bottom!

"Did you ever accept any money or gifts from her?" the Chief snapped suddenly, the angry eyes under glass fixed on him.

The blood rushed crazily to his head and he stared blindly at the Chief. Was he trying to accuse him of living off the proceeds of prostitution?

"No, sir—never," he said, his voice choked with anger.

"She said she gave you a cigarette lighter," the Chief prodded.

Steve didn't answer. Rusty hadn't left out a thing.

"Answer the question. Did she give you a cigarette lighter?"

"Yes, sir, she did," Steve said, slowly. "I threw it away."

"You threw it away," the Chief mimicked.

"Yes, sir."

"She give you anything else—money or gifts?"

"No, sir."

"You're sure? Remember I can dismiss you from the force for lying."

"Yes, sir, I'm sure."

The Chief sat back and growled, "I don't want men like you on the force, Hochuli. You're a disgrace to the uniform. I'm suspending you right now for conduct unbecoming to an officer and for the good of the service."

Steve nodded, his face ashen.

"Put your shield and gun on the desk."

Steve obeyed automatically.

The Chief pushed the shield and gun to the stenographer.

"Take these with you," he instructed. "This man is suspended from the force as of now. Write up the complaint and give it to him before he leaves."

"Yes, sir," the stenographer said.

"Another thing. Have his service revolver picked up at his home."

"Yes, sir."

The Chief dismissed the stenographer with a wave of his hand.

"Stand up, Hochuli," the Chief said.

Steve stood stiffly at attention.

"Turn around and face the men, *swordsman!*"

Steve turned around and faced the eleven men.

"Here's a guy who thinks he can do anything he damned well pleases because he's a cop. Well, he's not a cop anymore.

He's suspended and when I get him to the Trial Room they'll throw him off this man's police force so fast it'll make his head swim."

Steve stared at a distant wall.

"If there are anymore swordsmen in this group, I strongly recommend they quit right now before I find out." He looked the men over searchingly. "Back on duty and do your job out there!"

The men filed silently from the room.

Steve turned and tried to speak. "Sir, I ..."

"Get out," the Chief snarled, rising from behind the desk. "I'll see you at the Trial Room."

Steve stumbled to the door. The falling sensation had stopped as suddenly as it had come. He had hit bottom.

But he still had his life to live, even if he had to start it over. And he knew there had been eleven men in that room who would never forget Rusty, never forget the legs they had seen when she had slipped up her skirt or the breasts they had seen through her open satin blouse, would never forget her twisted smile or her large blue eyes or her red hair or the way she walked and talked. And they would never forget either why she must be booked and convicted again and again until the last time. He knew Rusty and he knew the men, and he felt a little better, as he walked from the room and closed the door behind him.